Other Books by Deborah Levy

Ophelia and the Great Idea

Beautiful Mutants

Swallowing Geography

The Unloved

D0096054

billy

and
girl

a novel by

Deborah Levy

Dalkey Archive Press

Originally published in England by Bloomsbury, 1996
Copyright © 1996 by Deborah Levy
First American edition, 1999

Library of Congress Cataloging-in-Publication Data:

Levy, Deborah.
      Billy and Girl / Deborah Levy. — 1st American ed.
           p.   cm.
      ISBN 1-56478-202-6 (alk. paper)
      I. Title.
PR6062.E9255B55   1999
823'.914—dc21   98-49257
                                              CIP

This publication is partially supported by a grant from the Illinois Arts Council,
a state agency.

Dalkey Archive Press
Illinois State University
Campus Box 4241
Normal, IL 61790-4241

visit our website: www.dalkeyarchive.com

Printed on permanent/durable acid-free paper and bound in the United States
of America.

For Jessica

Part One

1

Billy

Soon all the kids in England will be pushing up daisies.

That's what Girl says every night before I go to sleep. Girl is my sister and I'm scared of her. She's seventeen years old and got ice in her veins. Tonight she reads me my rights.

'Billy,' she says in that voice like turps, 'you have the right to complain about the weather. You have the right to promote Billy products when you're famous. You have the right to help me find Mom and you have the right to tell me what happened to Dad. Which one is it to be?'

Yesterday she bought me a present. A pair of stacked red trainers wrapped in folds of white tissue paper. She likes me to look like a baby gangster and I don't mind, but now I have to pay for them. My sister pretends to be retarded sometimes so she doesn't have to speak or react like other people do. Just as you think she is in Neverland, she suddenly springs on you with her white-trash fists.

Girl was in love once. She was nice to me then and bought me a badminton set for us to play in the park. Love made her high enough to sing and jump and swipe the shuttlecock back to me with the toy racquet. Her sweetheart was called Prince. He bought me a water pistol and I shot myself in the ear, up the nostrils, in my heart, on the inside of my thigh, dying for the neighbourhood cats with their spacey eyes.

*   *   *

'Which one are you going to choose, Billy?' Girl's black eyes always vacant, conveniently giving the impression she is brain-damaged. I am in the womb of my mother who will later disappear without trace. 'Don't cry,' Girl chides me, twisting her thin lips.

I am in the womb of my mother. I hear car alarms go off and sometimes I hear my father. He says, 'Hello, babykins. This is your daddy speaking. We are looking forward to meeting you, over and out.' I hear cats purring and Girl shouting, 'You're late, brother. Come on out!' I don't want to be born. I'm never coming out. Dad tries again: 'Hello, babykins, it's your daddy here. Time to face the world like a man – look forward to meeting you, son. Over and out.'

Mom used to stroke my head, babying me. I'd like to eat something with onions in 'em. Pizza or soup. Like Mom used to make before she disappeared. The night before she birthed me, she swam in shorty pyjamas and ate cinnamon buns. Life could have been amazing. We could have gone together to the video shop and bought ice cream, jelly beans and micro popping corn. We could have sat at home and watched a film, sprawled on the floor, stuffing ourselves.

Girl says, 'No, Billy, that is someone else's memory. We never went to a video shop.'

Yes, we did. When RoboCop says, 'Stay out of trouble,' I listen to him, but the trouble is in my head. It's in my chest and the back of my neck. After I was born I howled the hospital down. I howled like the heart that had taken nine months to grow was going to splatter onto the silver stainless-steel tray the midwife was holding nearby just in case.

*   *   *

I can see myself clearly as I was then. This is how I came to be Brother Billy in the English climate. I started life as a cell. The male and female chromosomes are fusing. I am two cells. Now I am a cluster of cells. Suddenly I am a tiny embryo embedded in Mom's uterine wall. Four weeks old and I'm two millimetres long. I have the beginnings of a nervous system. No fingernails to chew yet. My hands and feet have ridges which will become fingers and toes. A spinal cord has begun to form. Ten weeks and my kidneys have started to produce urine. I weigh eight grams, like a little packet of mince. By the end of the third month I've grown a forehead, little snub nose and a chin. Watch out, family, cos my lips are beginning to move. I'm never coming out. Even to have a go at them. I'm not going to arrive. I wrinkle my forehead in preparation for sorrow and disgust. I'm learning how to swallow and breathe. Mom is being sick on Dad's best Elvis-style shirt. Afterwards she guzzles salt and vinegar crisps helped by Girl who's always got her sticky white fingers in the bag. Twelve weeks old and I can hear her sharp little teeth crunching crisps. I can hear Mom's heartbeat. I can hear her blood whooshing. Mom is crying and Dad is crying. Girl just snivels. I can hear doors banging. Eighteen weeks old and I want to retire. That's a long time to live in my book. I've had enough. No such bloody luck. Mom keeps on eating and I keep on growing. I'm sucking my fingers in fucking dread. Oh God. I can taste something. Dad does his rocker's croon. 'Hell-oo, Babykins – we're going to call you Bill-ee!' Mom tells Dad she wants him to leave the house and never come back. My eyes are tight shut. I am six months inside Mom and if I was born now I might survive out of her body. I want a good-looking woman lawyer who loves children to take my case to the European Courts. I've got toenails. Mom tells Dad I'm pressing against her bladder and she got caught short. Dad laughs and strokes her belly. That's when I open my eyelids and start to kick. Eight months and my testicles began to descend into the scrotum. I got hiccups. Why? Because Mom's producing adrenaline. It's flooding into the bloodstream. She's frightened. Her fear is leaking hormones into me: I am in biochemical harmony with Mom and I got fear in me too. Now my fingernails have reached the fingertips. I'm going down now, head first. I got a lot of fat laid down ready for the world. Girl is singing something horrible. Mom's got sweet stuff in her breasts waiting for me. Yep, for me. Billeeeeee! Thing is, I won't be coming out to taste it. Oh, no. The weather will be cool out there, I know it. I don't want to arrive. No No No No. Oh God, *no*! The midwife pats Mom's forehead with a towel. 'He'll give in, don't worry, love. He's got the whole family to meet, hasn't he?'

.Leave out the formal introductions, won't you. I'm sure the family will make themselves known to me in their own good time.

All normal infants are supposed to smile, aren't they? Laughter is genetically coded into the body. I'm slapping my little white thighs and chortling already.

Dad pulled into a petrol station. He put the pump into his mouth and got five pounds' worth. Then he took out his pack of cigarettes and lit up. It was the biggest barbeque south London had ever seen. My father had never smoked before. This was his first and last cigarette and his suicide was the most splendid thing he ever did in his life. Girl and I have talked about it over and over. We decided he must have bought the pack from the newsagent near the Odeon. Coins cold in his hand. Black secret in his heart. Streatham's lone cowboy without horse or bourbon, just an imagination never expressed until now. All the people coming out of the Esso shop clutching sausage rolls and cans of Fanta fell

6

about screaming. A reporter from a newspaper offered Mom the chance to 'open her heart to the world'. Afterwards she bought Girl a Cindy doll with long blond hair, a blue bikini, a little pearl necklace and a plastic Ferrari with silver wheels. We set fire to Cindy one night and watched her melt in front of our eyes. Then I went off to watch Looney Tunes outside the TV shop in the mall.

After I was born Mom took special painkillers because they cut her up at the hospital to pull me out. Remember I didn't want to come out. They cut her and then told her to cross her heels like a cat. 'Cross your heels like a cat,' the midwife said, and yanked out the placenta with both hands. I lay on Mom's breast and they stitched her while Dad cried in the corridor, eventually putting his head round the door and whispering, 'All right, pet?'

Why don't they all do something about my 'welcome to the world' breakfast? Like a smorgasbord of analgesics and a razor blade?

When Mom took me home she examined my fingernails first. 'Look, Girl,' she said, 'they've grown right to the edge and over.' So I would scratch my face with my sharp nails. Make little fists and raise them to my cheeks and scratch because it upset Mom and made her kiss me more. She'd sit in a blue bucket under the shower, the smell of lavender she had added to the water filling the steamy corridor where Girl and I sat waiting for her. 'The lavender fields of Provence, Billy, that's what you can smell,' she shouted through the steam, and Girl and I watched the rain splash against windows, shivering in our second-hand T-shirts.

After she had bathed her birth wounds and done her hair – Mom wore a beehive that Dad said was a bit like Priscilla Presley

– she limped downstairs to make Girl breakfast: banana fritters. Girl wanted banana everything. Banana milkshakes, banana blancmange, banana curry. Mom was a bit nervous of Girl and catered to her compulsions for fear her daughter would weep those catastrophic tears of hers and never stop. When Girl cries the world slows down. It's like her thin white body is going to snap in two because her grief is so total and infinite. In the days we used to go for drives into the country, if she didn't see a horse she'd scream and shout as if somehow this was a bad omen and the sky was going to fall on her head. Dad would get desperate and point to a cow grazing in a field. 'There's a horsie, Girl, see?' The lie seemed to comfort her, as if just naming the beast completed the magic circle in her ash-white head, and she would calm down and fall asleep.

Girl has always invented games for me and her to play together. Her favourite used to be the Bolt Game. When she found a jar full of two-inch wrought-iron bolts in the cupboard under the stairs where all the nails and screws were kept, she showed them to me as if she had found gold in a cave. All day she brooded on what to do with them, hiding behind her fringe of ash-white hair when anyone dared speak to her. 'It's a pain game, Billy,' she whispered when Mom went out of the room and the next thing I knew she had dragged me outside and was drawing a chalk line on the pavement which I had to stand behind. Then she measured twenty footsteps away from my line and drew another line which she stood behind. The idea was I had to keep completely still while she aimed the little bolts at my head. When they missed and got me on my shins or on my fingertips I was not allowed to cry. It was a pain game, after all, and success was measured by how stoic the person being hit could be. What would it be like never to feel pain? The day Girl broke the skin on my forehead and blood dripped down my face and onto my T-shirt, she screamed, 'Don't blink, Billy!' and then hugged me for being well hard. When I pretended not to feel pain, I know that Girl felt it on my behalf. 'You're a hero,' she said in her acid-drop voice, and licked the warm blood with her tongue while I pretended to meow like a kitten. Girl's pain game prepared me for being bashed by Dad. Girl was training me up to receive pain. It was her way of protecting me. My very own personal pain trainer. The first time Dad smashed his fist into my kidneys I was seven years old. Mom was out and Girl was in. I hollered and my sister went very quiet. She smoked her first menthol cigarette then. Coughing but no words.

A few weeks after Dad set fire to himself at the petrol station, Mom took me on a coach trip somewhere near Newcastle to meet my grandfather. That's my mother's father. She packed tuna sandwiches and a flask of tea and sat me on her knee in the coach even though I was ten years old, so she wouldn't have to pay for another ticket. I swear I could smell rubber on the tarmac of the motorway and the lacquer in Mom's hair and when we arrived we heard a fat man in a pub sing, 'England! Awake! Awake! Awake!' I sat under the little tartan blanket and scratched my eyelids, all the time remembering my dad whispering, 'Hell-oo, babykins, it's your father here, over and out,' scratch scratch, and Mom catching my fingers tight in her hands. Grand-Dad talked in whispers to Mom, sometimes leaning over me with his watery eyes and beery breath, checking me out and looking away again.

I swear by the time he had cracked three bad jokes, I thought, Jeez, I really need a fag.

'You are my balaclava angel,' Girl whispers to me as I hold up the mirror for her while she trims her fringe. No, I'm not. I'm

9

a broken-hearted bastard. I want to be the bloke in the Haägen Dasz ads, with good-looking girls in their underwear pouring ice cream all over my big beautiful body. Instead I'm poor, white and stupid. I take my knife into cinemas and stab the velvet seats in the dark. That is my silent broadcast to the British nation. Pain is like lager and Elastoplast. It has made me who I am. There is a history to my pain. It is an experience in search of an explanation but I can't remember what the experience was. There ain't no ointments, surgery or insurance form going to heal my nerves and neurotransmitters. The making and unmaking of pain. Grief is like pain. Sometimes it's hard to experience them apart. I still feel it along the pulses. You can excite pain by touching the parts that hurt. That is what we are going to do.

At night I hide in small gardens outside here and count the TV aerials. I click the heels of my new red trainers three times, take a deep breath, hold my nose, and wait for the wind to take me somewhere better than this.

2

Girl

Why did the chicken cross the road? Because its mom disappeared and its dad set fire to himself. What that skunk Billy doesn't understand is that pain is not a riddle. It's a mystery because we lack crucial information. Billy's skin is blue. In all weathers. Indoors and outdoors. Blue like the soil on Jupiter probably is. If they ever put Billy into a spaceship and spin him up to the planets, I know he'll feel at home so long as he can take the TV and a stash of popcorn with him. I bought him a cowboy shirt to keep him warm. It's got pearl buttons and an extra one sewn inside the cuff in case. Billy always checks the emergency button is still there when he puts it on. It comforts him just about more than anything else. He wants an emergency button for everything: to get out of nightmares, to call for help when the lift gets stuck, to get out of boring conversations.

Got a tattoo inked into his scrawny upper arm. An old-fashioned one like some virgin boy sailor who called men 'sir' and choked over his first Lucky Strike in a foreign bar full of hookers. I mean, I can't believe he had that dopey tattoo done like all the other fat blokes in the world. It's an anchor entwined with roses and doves. It says Mother, of course.

I don't know why my mother called me Girl.

Sometimes I think she was just too lazy or too depressed

to bother calling me by my proper name, Louise. So there are two of me: one is named, the other unnamed. Louise is a secret. No one knows about the Louise part of me. Girl stuck and that's how it's always been. Louise is England's invisible citizen and when I read statistics about how many people live in this country, I always add one more: Louise.

When I was seven, instead of learning the times tables off by heart I learnt the name of every single cleaning product. My mother didn't want a daughter, she wanted a slave girl. Instead of running through parks in little black patent shiny shoes and green ribbons on the end of my plaits like girls do in storybooks, I ran about the house in my knickers with a dustpan and brush. My hands were always in bowls of dirty water washing plates or tying knots in black bin liners full of rubbish. The day I sat my art O level at school all the other kids brought in bowls of fruit and vases of flowers to sketch in charcoal for the still-life exam. I brought in a J Cloth and an aerosol of furniture cleaner and signed my drawing 'Girl'.

Billy never had to lift a finger. Not only was my brother given a name, but my mother used to dab lavender behind his ears even though he looked like a cocky little evangelist from the day they tore him out of her body at the hospital. Listen, I am no slave girl. I want to be a love diva.

Thing is, no one has ever taught me how to kiss.

Louise is waiting for her prince. He will find her, and gallop towards her on a horse. Every single horse in England must be counted so that Louise will recognise the steed when it comes towards her; she will point and say, 'Of course I knew it was going to be that one, the fine white stallion I saw in Kent from the car window.' They spoke silently to each other through the glass of the window and Louise knew she had chosen him and he was destined to find her. Girl says, 'You really make me puke lizards, Louise. I'm going to cut your long hair with nail scissors. I'm going to cut the horse into steaks and eat it raw. I'm going to carve DANGER into your arm with glass. Listen: the spirit of the Horse and Prince have got into the hollow tubes of your nervous system. It's a conspiracy. It's a bacillus like tuberculosis, wheeze and cough it out of your body now!' But Louise doesn't listen. She's waiting for the big day. The prince is Dad.

Dad topped himself. He was a lorry driver and used to show me the big teddy bear he'd hung up in the cabin for good luck. After he died we had to throw away his clothes. The sleeves of his favourite Elvis-style shirt spread out like Christ on the cross. A hero. A saviour. A king. I've forgotten how he died. Oh God. Bring my father back to me, safe and sound. Give him back his face. Give him a salary so he can do a weekly shop. Let him buy me a snooker table for Christmas. Give him spirit (hope) so I might catch some of it. Give him electricity (light) so I might see him. Give him words so he might speak to me in my hour of need. Give him another chance so that he can spread honey on my white-bread sandwiches. Give him back with a brand-new skin cleansed of pain, but mostly give him back with a wad of tenners in his back pocket, because that will make him happiest and he can drink a pint without fear in his heart. A poor man is wrapped in pain.

After Dad got burnt, my mother took Billy to visit Grand-Dad in Newcastle. 'He's got a glare in his eye, your boy,' the old clown wheezed when he caught Billy's stare and found himself trembling. My mother just stroked his forehead like she always did, mad about her boy. She cried over his bruises. Dad said he'd never hit his son again. But it was like Billy encouraged him. Even when he was a baby he was doing pain research. Crazy for Billy. When Mom disappeared, Grand-Dad was supposed to come and look after us. He did for a while. And then, all of twelve years old, I told him to go. We couldn't stand his jokes. Ever been to Ducksworth? How much are you worth? It was more than I could bear. Knock knock. Who's there? You. You who? Yooohoooo! A month of that sort of grief I suggested he go home, which is what he secretly wanted to do – and just send us money instead. We did not want our young minds damaged by Grand-Dad humour. 'What's the point of having shampoo when you can have real poo?' It's a good thing Grand-Dad left sharpish. Better to have his cash every week and draw him little pictures on thank-you paper.

I love my brother. He is a crippled angel, flying and falling seven days a week. This boy is a genetic engineer because ever since our mother disappeared, he invents a new mom to love him every night. Read his beautiful lips. Ready steady go!

Yeah. Horrible, isn't it?

Billy smells of Colgate and chips. Sometimes he burns a cork and draws a little moustache on his upper lip. This is his manliness. I mean, who is he supposed to have learnt how to be a man from? Not Dad, that's for sure. But Billy, who might never become a man, only a play man, a parody of a man, is going to win me and him a new world. A world without pain. Is that possible? Christ, sometimes I wish I had rheumatoid arthritis and a sweet young nurse would explain it was a chronic degenerative condition and send me to physiotherapy twice a week. Pain is the suburb of knowledge we grew up in. Little houses crowded together, narrow streets and dodgy lampposts. Pain has unanchored us, sent us raging down the nerve pathway to Patel's English and Continental Groceries for chocolate bars.

3

'Why're you so hung up on this pain thing, man?' Raj often has to stop himself creasing up at Billy. The boy's small for a fifteen-year-old, comes up to Raj's waist, close enough to admire the buckle on his belt. Raj is convinced Billy is going to be famous for something, he's just got that look about him. Like he's grooming himself for fame.

'I'm telling you, Raj, my sister's not the only one who gets upset around here. Do you know that word, Raj? *Mad?*'

Now that Raj is doing a part-time mechanics course he only works three days a week in his father's shop, Patel's English and Continental Groceries. Billy likes a good chat to Raj. For a start, the shop is just a short walk to the end of his road and Raj is a trapped audience. He can't walk out when he's bored.

'How come you know the word "Whiskas", Raj, but you don't know the word *Mad*? Pain is an event that demands interpretation. That's why I go on about it. I'm writing a book, as I've told you many a time in the Pickled Newt.'

'Yeah?' Raj looks genuinely impressed. Sometimes he takes Billy for a half at the Pickled Newt and gives him a problem to solve. The boy likes to think of himself as an expert on the human mind and it's true he's always got his nose stuck in a book. He stretches his hand out to the biscuit shelf and opens a packet of Jaffa Cakes. Better feed Billy England up, then. He hasn't got a mum to cook for him, has he? 'What's it called?'

'*Billy England's Book of Pain.*'

Raj methodically chews all the chocolate off his Jaffa, waving the packet in Billy's direction. The boy shakes his head, deep in thought.

'I should have gone to university when I was six. The study of the mind is my life's work. I should have read books in libraries, not been stuck at home making milkshakes for Girl. Made notes in the margins. Underlined sentences with my little pencil stub. I should have gone on dates with girlfriends.'

Raj wants to shut the shop and go for a pint. It's been a long day, especially as Stupid Club, that being the local neighbourhood community, have used the shop to debate their topics all day. They stand in a huddle by the fridge pretending to buy a packet of sugar, discussing why it is that some people wash dishes and then don't think to rinse them. So when you make yourself a sandwich, right, and you put it on a side plate that hasn't been rinsed, the bread tastes of the washing-up liquid. This is just one of the many topics debated by Stupid Club on a daily basis. Raj's father once tried to freeze the club out of his shop by turning off all the heating. His family went down with a strain of killer flu and Stupid Club rose to the occasion. Shuffled into the shop wrapped in extra woollies and hats, slapping the tops of their arms, united and cheerful, while his children and wife shivered in bed on antibiotics.

'I've missed out, Raj! I should have been nervous when I had a haircut case my girlfriend didn't like it. We should have gone to the movies together and shared a packet of chocolate raisins. We could have gone to Phuket for a fortnight! Instead I'm holed up here with my crazy bitch sister.'

Raj is interested in the crazy sister. Not many good-looking seventeen-year-olds in the street. 'Don't forget her menthols.' He slaps down a pack of ten cigarettes with pictures of eucalyptus trees laden with snow on the box. 'A present from me. Tell her to pop in, I haven't seen her for a while.'

'Shall I tell you where she is?' Billy knows that Raj is always interested to know where Girl is.

'Where?'

'Doing a Mom check.'

'What's a Mom check?'

Billy decides to chew on a Jaffa after all. 'It's where she knocks on the door of a house and pretends that any woman who comes to the door is our mother.'

'Yeah?'

'Sad.' Billy guffaws.

'Why do you say "Mom"? That's American, isn't it?'

'Watching telly. We like American sitcom moms.'

Raj nods, bewildered. It's quite nice to feel bewildered, makes a change from Stupid Club reading out loud the nutrition information on plastic tubs of margarine.

4

The A27 is a circular road that goes around London. A three-lane carriageway. The sky is grey and the tarmac is grey. Girl asks the cab driver to stop for a while so she can look at the 1930s houses built on the shore of the highway. Pebble dash. Old-fashioned flowers growing in the front drive. Tall purple gladioli and trimmed bushes of honeysuckle. Latticed windows. A shining car parked in each well-swept drive.

'Thinking of buying a property then?' The cab driver smirks behind his hand.

When Girl winds down the window the lever falls off. Foam stuffing oozes out of the back seat. Rusting springs poke into Girl's hips. 'Your car's a fucking lousy pile of shit.'

The driver can't decide whether she's a rock star or a psycho. 'Don't worry about it,' he says, just to be on the safe side.

'I won't.' Girl suddenly opens the door of the cab and a rush of dust flies into her face.

'Mad cunt.' The driver leans towards her trying to keep his hands on the wheel as the door comes off its beaten-up hinges. It drags down on the tarmac and Girl jumps out, skipping between the traffic until she makes it to the other side. The Other Side is important to Girl. She always wants to make it to there.

Girl strides in her silver loafers right up to the driveway of the biggest house in the street and thumps on the door with her fists. Then she rings the bell. While she waits she takes out a pack of menthol cigarettes and lights up. Her face is pale. It always is, but today it is especially pale. Every now and again she bends her knees and peers through the brass letterbox. Girl takes a deep drag of menthol. As far as she's concerned, menthol is a painkiller. A painkiller with a bit of glamour. She pushes away her peroxide-blond fringe and straightens up. Someone coming. God, she's so slow. Come *on*!

'Hello, Mom,' Girl says loudly to the middle-aged woman staring at her from behind the door. What a fucking hideous sight.

Dirty pastel-pink fake-fur slippers. Summer dress patterned with faded rosebuds and threadbare red robins. Plump arms covered in a peppermint-green cardigan, most of the buttons missing. Band of gold on the finger of left hand. A fucking thick band of gold. The woman shoves her hands into the pockets of her cardigan and gasps when the fabric crackles, sending little electric shocks into her fingertips. Her mouth is open wide, gaping. Girl observes that Mom's teeth are white and straight. Well looked after. Landscaped. Cleansed by a hygienist. Filled with white porcelain. Bleached and filed.

'Who does your teeth, Mom?' Girl drops her menthol cigarette on the doorstep and stubs it out with the toe of her silver loafer. The woman just stares. She starts shaking her head, very slowly from side to side, her hand rummaging for something in her pocket. A piece of tissue stained with pink lipstick. She brings it to her lips as if to catch something in her mouth, something unpleasant she has chewed and wants to spit out.

'Billy is quite well but not all that well, thank you, and I am as you see me.'

'Don't shout.' The woman can't quite bring herself to plead, but her eyes are scanning the neighbours' windows, sealed off from the busy highway with cream-coloured lace.

Girl opens her mouth wide like she's going to scream the house down.

'I won't scream, Mom. I promise. Why would I do a thing like that?'

Something flickers in the woman's B-movie eyes. Jeeezus. Girl keeps her face blank as she can, but it's really hard. You'd have to be a serious cultist to appreciate this Mom. It's like she's beginning to come to life, some sort of life, a dazed Nembutal life. She's definitely breathing, that's for sure. Got an appetite too. A little chocolate biscuit in her pocket. She's even got a smell. Cologne. Foul swabs of sweetness coming from Mom. Druggy sweetness, dirty fake-fur sweetness, tissues stained with spit and melting chocolate. Little pearls in her ears. Oh God. She's wringing her hands. Lips trembling.

Girl stares into the bronze dolphin doorknob. 'Just driving down this way to do a bit of shopping, Mom. Thought I'd call in.'

'I have no recall,' the woman says slowly, a slight West Country twang to her dopey voice.

'Where do you shop then, Mom?'

'FreezerWorld.'

'Really. How interesting. And what do you buy there?'

'Herrings. For my husband.'

'But what do you buy for yourself, Mom?'

The woman scratches her forehead absent-mindedly. Her cheeks are lightly dusted with powder. Sweet. Mom's gone. Even though she is standing there breathing, she is gone.

'I like profiteroles,' she says eventually.

'Profiteroles! *Dangerous* things to eat, aren't they, Mom? Bite into it and all that *cream* oozes out, gets stuck in your nostrils and you can't breathe, can you, Mom?'

The woman's pleading eyes. Little beads of sweat gathering in the corners of her faint moustache.

21

'Do you have a message for Billy?'

This takes some time to go in. Worm its way into Mom. Layers and layers of Mom. Almost there.

'It's his wedding anniversary, is it?' Mom looks proud of herself.

'Yeah? Billy's fifteen, Mom. Do me a favour and call me a minicab.'

The woman suddenly looks more alert. It's as if she can relate to this request. She nods and shuffles off in her pink fake-fur slippers, deeper and deeper into the thick pile carpets.

A white Mercedes parked nearby has its engine running. Not running, purring. A big white beast licked clean and shiny. Waiting for Girl. Actually waiting for her. Like he's been there all along, expecting her. An albino lion, muscled and gorgeous. The driver quick as a flash springs out of the Merc and holds the door open for her. 'Good morning, madam,' he says, as if they've known each other for years. He can just make out bits of his female passenger in the front mirror. First her peroxide hair. Then her cheekbones. Then her mouth.

'Where do you want to go, madam?'

'FreezerWorld.'

Girl makes two fists with her hands and thumps them into her eyes. The driver pretends not to notice the tears trickling between her fingers.

'We want to make your world a better world. That's why I'm going to tell a secret to everyone in FreezerWorld today. For those of you who like coffee we have a special offer on instant *cappuccino*. Buy any two items from the DIY section and you get a jar free! Yes, Cherie. Enjoy the taste of the continent in your own home.'

FreezerWorld. Open from 8 am to 8 pm every day. Painted a

dirty blood colour outside, but inside it's cleaner than a hospital. A man's voice announces bargains of the moment through invisible speakers. Customers carry Plant of the Month out to their cars, a wispy coconut plant. Struggling with it through the parking lots, making room in the boot, loading up their FreezerWorld goods.

Girl prowls the aisles. A desert of lino and weird light. She's a hunter. Looking for Mom. So many of 'em – moms. Shopping in Arctica. A frozen world. Girl needs a harpoon and an icepick. She needs to wear the skins and furs of the animals that lie packaged in the industrial freezers. And more. Beasts not eaten in England. Sealskins, polar bears and white Arctic fox furs. She needs working dogs for the hunt. Huskies. Crystals of ice caught in their paws. Odours of blood and fear. Weathering the storm without a compass. Looking for Mom. Big fucking girlprints through the snow.

But she's lost heart today. Not dressed for Frozen World. Not interested. Except for the girl in FreezerWorld overalls packing frozen peas into the industrial fridges. The way she holds the packets. Pressing the palms of her hands flat on each one of 'em. Cooling her hands as if her fingertips are on fire. Complete concentration. A man is walking up to her. Watching her. He's got a bit of power, that's for sure. FreezerWorld prestige. The manager. Yep. Little plastic badge on his red blazer tells the eager shopping public that he is 'Mr Tens'.

'Hello, Louise,' he says. 'You'll have to work a little faster than that.'

Mr Tens is a kind man. Not scolding Louise. Telling her a fact. Louise. Girl just can't bear to hear that name, though she knows lots of girls are called it. Mr Tens says something strange. Girl can't be sure she's even heard it right. Something like, it's not your hands that are hot, it's in your head, Louise.

23

And Louise is nodding her silky head, her lips moving, sound coming out. 'I'm as stupid as a blonde can get,' she replies, working faster now.

FreezerWorld. Deep-freeze pain. Frozen World. Pain tics in ice blocks. Dolour. The frozen tumour twilight. Louise and FreezerWorld. Girl and FreezerWorld. An autopsy waiting to be interpreted. Call in the anaesthesiologists, biofeedback technicians, occupational therapists, neurophysiologists, dieticians, pain peripheralists and pain centralists. Girl and Louise. Both know something useless.

Knowledge that won't even buy them a week's shop. They know that childhood is a primitive culture. Soothing words can relieve pain and harsh words can kill you even though you're still alive, drinking Fanta, watching breakfast TV, saving up for a kitten in the pet-shop window.

Louise turns her back on Girl. Talking to Mr Tens. But she wants Girl to hear what she says. Girl feels it with her girl intuition, snarled in the whole Louise thing, her secret name, knowing with terror that one day she's going to have to give up Girl and own up to Louise. Louise is asking her supervisor something. Important stuff. 'I start on the tills this Saturday, don't I?'

Mr Tens is nodding. Looks proud of her. 'Yes, you are, Louise. We're going to start you on Express. Customers with just a few items in their baskets. See how you go and then we'll have a think about where to put you next.'

Louise stares at him blankly. Nods and looks down at the packet of frozen peas in her small hands. Like a saint. Saint Louise of the Frozen Peas. Stupid as a blonde can get. Louise is just girlmeat. FrozenWorld girlmeat. No wonder Mr Tens feels like a celebrity.

*   *   *

Cruising the aisles. Checking out the panic population in FreezerWorld. Girl feels safe here. She can mingle with complete strangers at any time of the day and not feel afraid. It's as if the Voice broadcasting FreezerWorld news can read her thoughts because suddenly, in the middle of announcing a discount on mixed nuts and raisins, the Voice goes on a little detour.

'In winter when it gets dark early and certain neighbourhoods are out of bounds at 4 pm, FreezerWorld is well lit and warm. You are all here because you care. You want to feed your families. To nourish your wee ones. To indulge those you love. To treat yourself. Or even to stock up for a party. Cheers, everyone! Have a safe journey home.'

A frozen warm world. Girl can gaze at anything she likes, for as long as she likes, without having to explain herself. If FreezerWorld was a suburb, Girl would move there. She makes her way to the DIY section and reaches for an aerosol of red spray paint, thinking about stopping for a McChicken burger on the way home and checking out the mothers who eat there with their kids. Seems to take hours to walk back to the tills. FreezerWorld is a big world. She's not going to stand in a long queue for one bloody item. Where's the Express Mr Tens was talking about? Girl takes a white envelope from her jacket pocket, feels to check how thick it is and then rips it open.

Jeeezuz. Not much cash this week. A note in Grand-Dad's shaky Biro scrawl tucked inside: 'I'll make it up to you next week. The two-thirty didn't come home. Love Grand-Dad. PS Has Billy got a girlfriend yet?'

Of course Billy hasn't got a girlfriend. Spends all his time reading pain books. Billy doesn't want girlfriends, he wants patients to practise on. Girl sometimes obliges if her brother makes her a banana Nesquik. Lies on the settee and says the first thing that comes into her head. 'Smoking causes fatal diseases.' 'Diesel.' 'Wonderbra.' Her brother asks her to join up her words into sentences, sitting where she can't see him, sieving through Girl material. He's working on Raj too. Except Raj refuses to lie down on the settee even though Billy has explained the ethics of his practice. Raj prefers to talk over a pint at the Pickled Newt and Billy, who doesn't really like pints, prefers halves, takes tiny sips, his mouth stuffed with peanuts so as not to give away his thoughts. That's his special technique. Peanut blankness. Raj loves it when Billy does peanut blankness. Specially as Billy, being fifteen, is not supposed to be in the pub anyway. Raj has to hide him in the darkest corner, away from the action, sit him down with his back to the publican while he orders the drinks. He never tells Billy that the halves are really lemonade shandy.

Jeeezus. Even Express takes a year. Girl suddenly recognises the Voice. It's that man who was talking to Louise. Mr Tens. Thanks, Mr Tens. Don't get too carried away with mackerel in mustard sauce newsflash reverie. Stick to what you can do best, i.e. raise retard stock on the FreezerWorld floor. Girl finally pays for her aerosol with Grand-Dad cash and calls up a minicab on Raj's mobile. He lent it to her for trimming his hair.

While she waits for the cab to arrive, dreading the moment she claps eyes on it, always disappointed and hurt about the minicab wrecks she's forced to ride about town in, she prowls around the car park shaking her aerosol. Just what she wants. A wall that thousands of shoppers have to pass by in order to enter FreezerWorld. Girl knows exactly what she's going to write with her red paint. She can do it with her eyes shut.

MOM CALL HOME. GIRL X.

5

Billy

Girl wears her famous tears like jewels. Like glass blown from grief. Each tear takes approximately five seconds to form in the corner of her eye. You've got to be careful when you ask Girl what she feels. Here goes.

> Say what you feel, Girl?
> Say what you feel
> You Nescafé slut
> You cruel baby wolf
> Say what you feel.

'I did a Mom check.'

'And?'

'Hopeless. She just stared at me and said, "I got no recall."'

'Well, maybe she was Mom, then?'

'Naaaaaa. She's someone's Mom, but not ours. She called me a Mercedes cab paid for on her account.'

'Did she look like our mom?'

'We don't know what our mother looks like, now do we? But she didn't sound like her.'

'Did you tell her about me?'

'Of course I did, Billy. I always do. I said Billy is well but not that well.'

'Next time you do a Mom check, tell her I'm sick and dying.'

'She wouldn't be interested,' Girl snarls. 'No one's interested in a loser.'

'Mothers are supposed to be interested when their children are sick and dying, for God's sake!'

'The worst thing,' Girl says incredulously, 'was that she was wearing a pair of cute slippers.'

'Cute?'

'Little pink furry things, really dirty. Like the fur on a gonk.'

'A gonk. That's the saddest thing I've ever heard in my life.'

'She was like us, Billy. She had no recall.'

'Then it *was* her!'

'No, it was not! I know just as well as you what Mom's like and *that* was *not* her. Just fuck off, you creep. Go away! Get out of my sight! Stab yourself! Go *away*! Die with the gonks!'

I am blotting paper for Girl's anger. She takes it out on me and even more of it out on herself. It's just too much. If they ever make a robot Girl they'll have to give her tear ducts.

Click the heels of my red trainers three times. With force. Take me away from here. Take me home. That's what Dorothy Oz said to her dog. But this is home. Girl is full of junk and dirt and chemicals. Dead birds float on their backs in the slime. It's good for her to cry.

I know this because I read books about it. I study the mind and it's my life's work. Hopefully one day beautiful blonde mad girls will come to my couch and tell me their problems.

My consulting room will be a laboratory of the human psyche. My couch will become famous. Girls will sell their most precious belongings to afford my mind. Biographers will fight amongst themselves to describe my methods. 'He told lies. He told the truth. He gulped for air. He clutched his chest.' Perhaps I'll call myself Billy England. When I die, the world will be able to buy archive photographs of Billy England. The Billy poster, mug, tiepin, watch, pencil, cuff links, notepad. Billy portrait by Ralph von something. *The Diaries of Billy England.* Hardback. Paperback. A picture of Eros on the cover (he'll look a bit like Girl) – Eros the basic life instinct. Eros from sometime BC. That will soon change. First there was Before Christ. Then there was BB. Before Billy.

Girl and her Mom checks. Look – Mom disappeared when I was ten years old. I am now fifteen and she's not around to see how good-looking I turned out. Girl's looked after me ever since she turfed Grand-Dad out on account of his pathetic jokes. She was twelve at the time. We had a Girl and Billy conference and agreed he had to go. It's not good for the young mind to have to endure the wit of the senile. Girl's always known that I am special. Now that she's seventeen she would do the same thing over again. Boot out the clown. She did not want to see me contaminate my integrity by pretending to laugh at the moronic. Being looked after by Girl is one thing. An envelope full of Grand-Dad cash every week is okay. But Mom's not here to watch Wimbledon with. She's not here for her boy. That's not easy to say. She's not here for her boy. 'Scuse me, I just got to stick my head under the cold tap or something.

She's just not here for her boy.

What am I supposed to do with the information? It's like bricks flying around in my head. An earthquake shattering the architecture. Walls falling down. Cars crunching into

29

other cars. Bridges collapsing. Shoot the messenger? The messenger is me. Employ a night nurse to inject me with morphine every time I think about it? Go on a serial killing binge? What about when I become a man? She won't be here either. Truth is, I'm frightened to grow up too much without righting things with Mom first. Pain is a permanent winter. I am a boy without a car. And I will be a man without a car. Nothing to protect me from the weather. Girl gets cabs. She really hates it when they send her an impersonation of what a car might be – that's dodgy protection – the best they can do, grudging, and it makes Girl mad to think they think it's good enough for her. I'd rather be in the sleet than that. But Girl is a girl and she needs minicabs to run her about. Even if the vehicle is a car trauma.

I know it's crazy but sometimes I think one day Girl will really find her. Mom will come to the door and Girl will know. There is one thing about Girl I just don't understand. We think Dad died horribly. But we're not completely sure. He might have survived the fire. Girl is nuts about Dad. I think she is. But she never goes out looking for him. She's afraid she might find him and then what would she do? Call the emergency services? The way Dad laid into my boy flesh, he might as well have scooped me off the floor, poured me into a jar and labelled it BILLY CHUTNEY. Not that I am complaining. Dad really loved Mom. And I made it my life's mission to steal Mom's love from Dad. It was working. He could never get near her cos I was always on her lap. My little hands on her breasts. My little tongue that had grown in her womb, stuck in her ear. Whispering. Kissing her a million times a day and she not minding the snot running down my face. Making sure I got up extra early every morning to crawl into bed between them. Resting my legs on her stomach. Playing with her hair. When Dad tried to stroke her cheeks, I sat on her face. When Mom made pizzas I ate the lot and Dad left most of his. Then I'd eat Dad's. Dad hated pizza. Said he liked to eat Elvis food. Cheeseburgers and peanut butter on crusty white. A big handsome bloke with hair, very proud of it cos all his mates were bald. Too handsome. What do you want a good-looking father for? I mean, if a boy has to choose a father he's not going to leaf through a male-model catalogue, is he? Dad was a looker and despite his Elvis thing he liked to muck about with recipe books to make banquets for Mom. But I *needed* pizza and Mom enjoyed making them for me. She sang while she made 'em and I sang with her, even though I knew I was going to suffer for it later. Every Mom pleasure equalled a Dad bashing. Mom knew this too so she made sure the good times were good. I think Girl found it hard to square loving a dad that hurt her brother. She couldn't help herself, though.

If someone had banged spikes into Dad's body, she'd still have cuddled up to him. Even if it tore her arm off.

6

Girl

Billy is making pizza like he thinks Mom used to make. I know it's just a recipe he got off the telly. The little brute took notes and even sent off for the TV book. Unless Mom is channelling to us via the Italian slob who does the pasta pizza programme on Tuesday nights – his fat finger always stuck in some sauce – I have to believe that Brother Billy is just Mom-fixated.

First he smears olive oil onto the base with the special Chinese bristles he bought. I'm not allowed to use it. Ever. One day I'm going to stick it up the cat's arse and leave it there. Then he grates garlic that he can't be bothered to peel and sprinkles it onto the dough with his chewed-up fingers. Anchovies come next. Sardines. Shrimps. Tinned mussels. Octopus. Tiger prawns. Whelks.

Why not go the whole damn hog, Billy! Create the ocean on pizza in one night! Crustaceans. Molluscs. Transparent spineless creatures with boggle eyes and cavernous mouths. Hideous turdlike sea cucumbers that inch blindly across the seabed munching plankton and sucking sand. Vast flapping manta rays with electric whiplash tails cruising the bottom two inches. Anything that glows in the depths. Anything that lurks in the deep. I'm a nonswimmer. Dad knew that. He knew I hated wet food. He bought me crisps by the bagful. They made me sleep tight. Anyway, listen to me, Billy: I am *not* hungry.

Billy puts his head right inside the oven when he tries to light it. He looks like a suicide case, swearing and striking matches. 'These matches are made in the fucking Czech Republic,' he whines and wheezes like he always does.

'Listen, Billy, I've taken away your rights tonight. The only right you have is to give me Take Two on Dad.'

'Okay. Here's Take Two on Dad. Ready?' Billy pours himself a glass of tap water. 'Jeezus, Girl. I'm drinking someone else's hormones. You know that?'

He rolls down his shirtsleeves. Shivering on account of the weather. The weather inside him, that is. Seems like it's begun to sleet. A thin layer of ice seems to be setting in. All motorists are warned. If you don't want a pile-up, drive slow. Better still, stay at home. Come off it – it's not that bad. I mean, don't advise the ships not to sail or anything. It's just sleet this time. I said *sleet*.

Billy's lips are blue, of course.

'Dad sells low-cost car insurance in the United States. On the telephone. That way the customer can't see the burns on his face. He lives in a motel. Like a wooden chalet with a small porch. It's got air conditioning and a TV. It's got a shower and a microwave. It's got a tacky carpet and a king-sized bed. In the mornings he collects his mail from a special box and in the evening he goes to a bar next to the motel for a whisky sour. Dad spends his day saying things like "You'll be surprised how much you can save. We have a quick streamlined service and our premiums are low." His voice is English and sincere. "I'll give you a quote over the phone and cover you on the spot if you like. There are no nasty surprises. You can take out cover without filling in a single form." Dad's got a little rhyme he turns over while they speak back to him. It goes something like, "Oh, thank heaven for the 7-Eleven." He always wears a smart suit and a sharp haircut. Weekends he drives his hire car to the ocean. Dad don't give a fuck about the ozone hole. He lies under the sun smeared in his Hawaii oil and reads paperback thrillers. When he's reached maximum heat he walks to the water, a bit shy because his body is getting old. That doesn't stop the girls looking at him, though. He's got two other kids now, Girl. Bessie and Julian. He built them a swing in the garden out of an old car tyre. Sees them twice a month now he's separated from their mother. But he don't love 'em like he does us. They're American kids. Tall with blue eyes and nice teeth.

'Sometimes he tries to remember what we look like. But he can't. He looks at pictures of English kids in the newspapers. Does my Girl look like that girl? Does Billy look like this boy here? He's lost his memory. Just like us. He's got the feeling but not the memory. Every evening when he sips his whisky sour, he takes his watch off and lays it on the table next to him. He loosens his tie and stretches his legs. He smooths back his hair and he keeps his eye on the big clock on the wall. Dad is waiting for something but he doesn't know what it is. He's waiting for us, Girl. He's waiting for you. When he takes off his watch it's to free something up. It's like the mechanism inside the watch is blocking his pulse. He eats chicken tacos with melted cheese and says his rhyme over and over: "Oh, thank heaven for the 7-Eleven." It's like a verse sent to him from God. Dad never dreams and he never cries. He likes his fried eggs sunny side up and he's given up searching for marmalade.

'Dad has given himself up, Girl. He's not the man you remember. He's not the man he was. He's someone else. Dad is no longer Dad.'

'I hate him. I hate him.'

'There's no "him" to hate. Dad doesn't know who he is. What is the "him" of Dad?'

'I hate him.'

'I know you do,' my brother lies, opens the oven door half an inch and peers inside. A sleazy pizza peep show.

'And I hate your fucking pizzas.'

Louise loves pizza. Any kind of pizza. Nothing makes Louise happier than to eat pizza. Thin crust, thick crust, extra cheese, yes please, she even thinks Hawaiian is just fine. Ham and pineapple chunks. Tropical. She smiles her white-teeth smile even when they put an egg on her pizza. Why, an *egg*, how strange and interesting! Her favourite, if she has a favourite because she just loves them all, is American Hot. Pepperoni! Wow! In fact she would like *extra* pepperoni on her pizza *and* an egg. If the pizza chains want to try out pineapple chunks and ham with the pepperoni and egg, then she's up for it. What's more, Louise likes to start with garlic dough bread before she eats her main order of pizza. She wants naked pizza first. If the pizza chains want to give her dough balls to accompany her garlic pizza slice, Louise would like to eat them too. That's how crazy Louise is for the pizza product. Louise is going to eat Billy's pizza with relish, happy to experience the marvels of the ocean on dough. She is going to chew on inky squid and kiss her fingers which she has formed into a small cluster as she brings them to her lips – a gesture of approval to Chef Billy learned from watching foreigners in sitcoms. *Bon appetit.* She is going to pour her and her brother a glass of cold beer. 'To us, Billy,' she says. 'To our family. Good luck to us all.' Louise has silky hair and glowing skin. Her voice is firm and all her teeth are straight. She is not afraid to be uncertain and have doubts. She is not afraid of the deep. Her bath towels are always warm from the electric rail. Louise is light-hearted. Louise is ready for love.

*   *   *

Louise is my real name but Girl has stuck. What kind of a girl is FreezerWorld Louise? Why did that man, Mr Tens, say the heat is in her head, not in her hands? I got to find my trainers and do another Mom check.

7

Girl is exploding in space. Her calf muscles are taut, stretched, her peroxide hair flying, her thin arms flailing, faster, faster, away from Brother Billy and his TV recipes that go horribly wrong. Away from the boy from hell who says all good chefs give a bit of themselves to every recipe. Billy who said if she wanted to run really fast she should wear a headdress of feathers for lightness, height and flight. Away from Billy who has just told her something devastating. He said that when Mom disappeared, her soul entered his body and now he is a man with a woman's soul.

As she speeds through the park she thinks about God and whether he is watching her. Girl thinks her main thought: soon all the kids in England will be pushing up daisies. To avoid her main thought she thinks about supermarkets: how the shining lino of the aisles and the bright lights and the promise of so much makes her feel dizzy and excited and sick. She wants everything. Girl actually feels a pain in her side, the wanting is so acute – when she stares into the industrial freezers she clutches her ribs. An icy mist floats up between her and the boxes of frozen cheesecake. She puts her hand into the freezer and feels the chill creep up her arm. Shopping pains: the adrenaline she feels when she runs is how she feels when she shops. Tranced out. Both activities take her breath away. She wants big cartons of vanilla-flavoured yogurt made in Germany. She wants jewelled collars for dogs she does not own, batteries, Scottish shortbread, tin openers, frozen trout wrapped in cellophane and packed on small white plastic trays, a shoulder of heritage lamb, jars of mayonnaise, bunches of Cyprus mint, Egyptian potatoes, shampoos to take the chlorine out of her hair, a three-pack of nylon tights. She wants a spit-cooked chicken from the deli section, fat loaves of white bread, slabs of Gouda and Cornish Cheddar, she wants frozen pizzas in boxes – not the pizza Billy makes – factory pizza with diced green pepper and sweetcorn. She wants tubs of raspberry and chocolate mint ice cream, bottles of sweet dessert wine, vacuum-packed Arabic coffee and refill bottles of garlic salt; she wants boxes of cereal with free gift plastic robots in them and bottles of fizzy sweet drinks, nail-varnish remover, a hairbrush, face creams and Belgian chocolates. Girl wants everything the market can give her to pass time and to fill time. She wants to be someone who has plenty. Even plenty of what she does not want. Girl runs and cries. She does all the verbs. She wants, she cries, she runs, she cries some more. Watched by God who, as far as Girl is concerned, is just heaviness in the sky.

A red-brick Victorian house stands parallel to the park where she runs. Girl has been interested in the house for some time. So how come the mother who lives there never opens the curtains? How come the *stoopid* wooden duck on the window shelf looks like the duck Mom bought Girl when she was eleven? What about the giant satellite dish attatched with bolts to the roof? Mom was crazy about TV. I mean, what kind of TV experience does this satellite citizen want? Is it to scour the world looking for her lost kiddies? What most interests Girl is a solitary pink baby's shoe that has stood on the wall outside the house for months now. The weird thing is that Girl has the other shoe. She's had it for years. Two silver buckles stitched on the side with ripped, faded blue striped soles. One day Girl nailed her pink baby shoe to a piece of wood so that she would never ever lose it.

As Girl speeds past the house, the thing she has always dreaded happens. A woman sticks her head out of the window on the top floor and screams. She just screams. Mouth open. Her auburn hair pulled tight into a ponytail. Girl doesn't know who she's screaming at, but that doesn't matter. Still running, she swerves a sharp left into the concrete garden at the front of the house and rings the doorbell. She is sweating and breathless and everything in her body aches. Worst of all, the tiny pink shoe has disappeared from the wall.

Girl waits. Pain in bricks. Pain in the sky. Pain in Girl. She licks her lips. They are dry and she wants them to be moist. Always. Her lips are there to be kissed. Her lips are kiss-me lips. Something is happening on the other side of the glass door.

Two small girls press their hands against the glass, staring at her. Girl puts her hand over their two tiny hands. They squash their noses against the glass. Girl kneels down and squashes her nose against the glass. The youngest, she must only be about one year, pushes her tongue against the glass. Girl presses her tongue against the glass. One of them shouts for her mother. The screaming woman.

'Yes?'

Girl makes her voice low and steady and calm. 'Hello, Mom.'

'What do you want?'

Girl has to lean against the wall, she is so shocked. The woman has a tattoo on her upper arm. A heart with doves. Doves. Wings spread, flying, hovering over the heart which has a name inked in the middle of it. Capital letters. Italics. BILLY. She's got fucking Billy needled into her flesh for ever. BILLY.

'What do you want?' The woman opens the door wider so she can get a better look at the pale blonde girl on her doorstep.

'I'm Girl,' Girl says.

'Yeah, I can see you're a girl. What do you want?'

'Just wanted to say Billy's okay.'

One of the girls smiles at Girl. Three little teeth poke through her bottom gums. Her mother picks her up and straddles her on her hip.

Girl can see that the woman's eyes are really beautiful. Green. Slanting up at the edges.

'I don't care if Billy's dead,' she says in a bored voice. 'I don't give a damn if he's lying under a bus. No pain is enough pain for that bastard. He can't hurt enough as far as I'm concerned. So tell whoever has sent you to bring me news about fucking Billy, tell them the only good news is that he's in casualty and there is nothing the doctors can do for him.'

Girl's eyes begin to fill. She combs her fringe into her eyes with her fingers.

'Anyhow. I just wanted to say hello, Mom.'

'I'm not your mum,' the woman replies in a matter-of-fact voice. She stands very still, looking at Girl and stroking the top of her little girl's head.

'I am not your mum,' she says again, but softly this time.

'I saw you running in the park,' the woman says.

Girl nods.

'I opened the window to have a laugh with the neighbour downstairs.'

'I thought you were screaming,' Girl says.

'I was laughing.' The woman just stares at Girl, all the time stroking her girl's hair.

'Nigh nigh,' the little girl coos.

'Night night,' Girl replies.

'I'm not your mother,' the woman says again.

'No. It's a mistake.' Girl bends down to tie up her shoelace because tears are dribbling down her cheeks. They wet the concrete doorstep which is splattered with white pigeon droppings.

8

When Girl comes back from her run, Billy is waiting for her. He watches her drink water, glass after glass. Her yellow minishorts are soaked in sweat. He watches her put on her silver mirrored shades so she does not have to *endure* him watching her. He watches her take a cloth and a bottle of all-purpose lemon cleaner and start wiping the skirting boards, one knee bent, one leg stretched out.

'Yes,' Billy says. 'Crazee but true. Mom disappeared and I inherited. Yep. I inherited her soul. That's me. I was born heroic Girl, a heroic boy child whose destiny it is to liberate the world from pain. My body is hard but I'm soft inside. You might wonder why I sleep so long? I sleep her sleep and I sleep my own. I sleep for two. I eat for two. I take vitamins for two. I am the first *boy* on earth with a woman's soul.'

Girl says, 'I did a Mom check on my run.'

'And?'

'She doesn't think I've got the right person.'

'What did she look like?'

'Young.'

'But Mom's not young now.'

'I know.'

'Why did you think it was her then?'

'She was screaming.'

'Lots of bloody people scream. That's how you know someone's alive and not dead.'

'She was screaming in my direction.'

'What was she like?'

'Didn't get to know her.'

'What was she wearing?'

'Jeans.'

'Mom never wore jeans.'

'She had two babies.'

'Mom can't have any more babies.'

'I said you were okay.'

'I'm not okay.'

'One day I'll get it right. Mom will come to the door.'

'Well, don't tell her I'm okay when she does. Do I look okay to you?'

Girl switches on the TV to drown out Billy's whining voice. A woman is having a heart attack in an ambulance. The scene cuts to the hospital corridor. A group of doctors run as they wheel the woman into the operating theatre. Someone with a mask over her mouth passes the surgeon a pair of rubber gloves.

'Listen, Billy.' Girl pauses just long enough to give him time to rant about the ammonia that he can smell in her bottle of lemon all-purpose cleaner: how it's taking the paint off the skirting boards, how it's giving him brain damage, how one day he's going to drink a whole bottle of the stuff and die in agony on his bed.

'What I am saying,' Girl interrupts, 'is that we are special and unique.'

'No, we are not.' He turns on her. 'We are morons.'

The surgeon starts to cut into the flesh of the patient's belly. Suddenly a machine monitoring the patient's heartbeat begins to beep. Lights flash. The nurse screams, 'Dr Taylor! She's fading out!' The doors of the theatre fling open and another squad of doctors crowd around the woman. Three of them fiddle with the machine while another pumps the woman's heart with his hands. Billy cries when they thump the woman's heart. He blubs into his shirtsleeves. Girl can only see the back of his neck shaking as Dr Taylor holds the dying patient in his arms.

'Look, Billy. I am a secret citizen called Louise. You are a boy with a woman's soul. We could make big bucks.'

'Oh, yeah. Like in a clinic somewhere?'

'The USA. We could do the chat shows there.'

Girl lunges for Billy. She punches him in the heart until he cries out for special Girl mercy. She sinks her teeth into his pulse and yells for bananas. She says she's hungry. Starving. There's nothing to eat in this goddamn madhouse.

Billy gasps, 'Dr Taylor, save me, save me!'

Girl laughs like she's going to die.

'We've *got* to get our airfare to California. *Now*! They'll appreciate us there. They'll hire us a car. They'll fill our pillow slips with cocaine. We might find out what happened to Dad. We might discover why Mom disappeared. We'll get a tan. We'll surf the big Pacific rollers. We'll eat T-bone steaks! We'll give them our pain and they'll give us their cash.'

'How we going to do it, then?' Billy's gone morose.

'We'll do a supermarket,' Girl declares emphatically, unusually animated, screwing up her fists. 'A *big* supermarket on the edge of a motorway. One that sells twenty types of frozen potato. Crinkle chips, steak chips, chilli chips, hash browns, yeah, hash fucking browns like we're going to eat in America. We'll crash into the tills and take the whole damn *lot*! We'll buy our air-tickets with supermarket cash. Ready, Billy? Are you ready for this?'

Billy thumps his pathetic pigeon chest like he's trying to revive his own dying heart, all the while thinking he might stroll down the hill past Arctic Wines, Junction Pets and the hair salon called Differences, for a half at the Pickled Newt. It's not the company he wants, it's the church next door to the pub that has inflamed him. The poster over the door that says, FIND REAL DIGNITY INSTEAD OF INCOMPREHENSIBILITY. Is his pain divine punishment? Life hurts more without magic. Will supermarket cash discover a hidden switch in the brain that turns off pain, once and for all?

'I've been ready all my life,' Billy replies in his sad boy voice.

9

Girl's head is full of Louise in FreezerWorld. Dark Louise thoughts. Following Louise home. Waiting for her at the end of her shift. Using Grand-Dad's weekly cash to buy Louise two plastic pink hair-slide hearts. Not giving them to her, of course. Keeping them for later. Writing her letters but never sending them. Dreaming Louise. Should she tell her brother about her Louise dream? Tell him everything? Risk him writing a book one day called *The Louise Dreams?* Because Billy's role from very young was fated to interpret pain on behalf of the Whole Happy Family. Even when he was in Mom's womb, Dad wanted to hurt him.

Okay. The Louise dream.
   There was a power cut at FreezerWorld. Water from the industrial freezers leaked a flood. The waters from frozen lamb and chicken livers and Irish-liqueur ice cream. Louise slipped and drowned. Louise is frozen girlmeat. A FreezerWorld product. A frozen girl. Trapped between sheets of ice. Nose and lips pressed against Frozen World. Golden ice drops of hair. Eyes staring, orbs of blue slush. Louise. Melting histories of retard pain. Chewed-up fingernails splayed against the ice sheets. Her hands so small. Like Girl's hands. Worst of all, she was wearing her FreezerWorld overalls, a little kilt underneath. All around Louise the customers had fallen into a deep sleep, slumped over their trolleys. Rows of little battery chickens on electric spits had stopped in midcycle. FreezerWorld Louise fallen in

so deep. The sight was terrible, monstrous. Girl wanted to die. The end of all hope. Girlmeat. But she had a choice. She could kiss the sleeping frozen Louise into consciousness. Undead her. Princess lips on princess lips. Break the ice.

The End.

FreezerWorld Louise, who is also Girl, is trapped in the ice age because she is frightened of the future. Which is the past.

Okay. Should she tell Billy about the Louise letters? Three of them so far. Written but not sent.

Dear Louise,
I followed you home from FreezerWorld. I know you know I am watching you. And I know you don't mind.
    Girl.

Dear Louise,
My name is also Louise. As far as I'm concerned all Louises have to be beautiful and have a grip. It's time you bought some different clothes. It's time you learnt some new words.
    I'm watching you, Louise.
    From Louise.

Dear Louise,
I saw you come home late the other night. Where were you?
I want to know. I hate your jacket, Louise. Denim is for losers.
You can only wear denim on a beach. Never ever wear denim in winter.
    Louise.

No. Girl is too alarmed to tell Billy her dream. She'd even prefer a Grand-Dad joke than confess how Louise has slid into her head like glass in a car accident. Girl knows that Louise is going to lead them to Mom.

On her secret visits to FreezerWorld she always makes her way to the Toiletries aisle to calm herself. Keeping an eye on Louise. Louise stocking shelves. Louise packing pork bellies into the freezers. Louise on the Express till. Louise talking to the manager, wringing her small white hands. Louise choosing a Valentine's Day card for her boyfriend, buying a Biro to write a message inside. 'To the Best Boyfriend in the World.' Chewing the pen. Risking a Bic biro heart, her initials, his initials, taking a deep breath, writing how her love is 4 ever, licking the envelope.

Girl likes the chemical fragrances of the FreezerWorld beauty products: musk rose, peach coral, ivory mist. The labels on the plastic bottles show pictures of desert islands and blue lagoons. The sky is always and everyone is happy always 4 ever. Peach Coral is where she wants to be. Peach Coral is her homeland to be. Girl is in exile and she wants to return home, even though she's never been there. A world where pain has been abolished and perfume bonds you with your loved one for ever. Babies giggling, plump and clean in the lovely arms of their mothers. It would be so sweet to be a resident in Peach Coral. To lounge in a hammock and read magazines all day. She wants to dream herself into peachness because she wants a happy ending. Like in the ads. Blue butterflies dancing on the backs of zebras. She wants to be there. Deep in Girl-land she thinks if they can dream it up, it's possible to get to the place where zebras canter into a sky full of hope and wonder. She would like to stroke one. The Adland fathers and grandfathers and aunts and cousins with their hopes and aspirations, their hairstyles and dialects. Putting a bit aside for a rainy day. Which is every day. Sometimes she gets scared that she's out of the picture completely. She wants to be there, inside the Ad family, well lit, well looked after. Girl wants it written in her passport: 'Country of Birth: Peach Coral.'

Even when Raj comes round she can't stop talking about FreezerWorld. Billy and Girl and Raj drinking Coke and then crushing the cans.

'What's FreezerWorld?' Raj always asks the important questions.

'It's a lovely world, Raj,' Girl makes her voice soft.

Girl smoking the menthols Raj filched from his father's shop. Inhaling snow on the tips of pine needles. Ice and clean cold wind burning up anger and hunger and memory.

'There are beautiful announcements in FreezerWorld.' Girl just won't let go. 'This voice announces things: "Have a safe journey home, don't forget to check out the Adidas trainers on special discount for your boys."'

'Who's the DJ then?' Raj reckons he should tell his father about the whole concept. They could try it in the shop.

'I think he's the manager. He says, "When you cut a FreezerWorld strawberry cheesecake, be sure to make a wish. Goodnight to all our loyal customers, may all your wishes come true."'

Billy is genuinely moved.

'Think I should say all that stuff?' Raj glugs down the rest of his Coke. "When you buy our special-offer bleach, be sure to drink it slowly. That way you make it last longer. Safe journey home, folks. Hope you don't fall under a bus."'

Girl is smiling now. She wants everyone to talk about FreezerWorld all the time.

'"Patel Continental and English groceries is a lovely world.

Why buy fresh lemons when you can buy them half dead? Why are they so expensive? Because they are wise lemons. They have seen life all right.'''

'I'll tell you what.' Girl is full of Raj-admiration energy. His interest in her kind of charges her up. She makes her voice casual, like what she's going to say is of no importance, just an idea to pass time. 'Let's all go to FreezerWorld. *Now!*'

Raj thinks about how sometimes Girl's black eyes look green. Green for *go*. Cross the road with mood in your shoulders, take your time, let the hooting vehicles know you're far away in your mind and they just have to wait. Her eyes are green now and she's stroking her fringe, agitating it with her fingers. He hands her his mobile to call a cab. Watching her punch in the numbers like she's calling an ambulance.

'I'll stay here.' Billy ignores Girl's axe murderer's stare. 'You can tell me about it later.'

'Billy, it's important that you come with us.'

'No. I got to bathe.'

'Do you remember what we were talking about?'

Of course her brother remembers what they were talking about. This morning he lay in bed imagining himself talking to a chat-show hostess with beautiful American teeth. He is saying, 'My father loved your country. He loved Elvis. He knew all the songs.'

The hostess, who is called Niki, folds her arms and gives her famous cheeky twinkly look straight to the camera. 'Billy, would you like to show us all how your father sang "Love Me Tender" in the kitchen when you were a little boy?'

'I'd like to be able to do that for you, Niki, but the thing is, he usually sang that particular song before he belted me, so I don't really feel in the mood.'

'Think that's our car hooting.' Raj puts his arm around Girl's shoulder. 'One day I'll have my own car and drive you about.'

Girl opens the front door. Screws up her eyes. 'That cab's a lousy pile of shit.'

'Why don't you tell him?'

'Cos he'll only say, "Had a bad day?"'

Billy screeches. Not exactly a laugh. More like a cat with its tail stuck in a door.

Her brother knows the warning signs. It's not like his sister is putting a message in a bottle and floating it out to sea. She's crashing a hatchet with words engraved on it right into his skull. The words say, 'We are going to *do* FreezerWorld.'

10

Billy

I hate the English weather. I don't see the point of smiling about something so tragic. The English people stop me on the streets and say, 'It's a bit rainy, if you know what I mean?' Well, I don't know what they mean because sometimes it's *not* raining. They say it even when the sun is shining. What the fuck are they talking about? Is it just always 'a bit rainy'? Even when it's not?

I'm young. My teenage bones need sun verbs, not damp. You buy a sausage, one hundred per cent heritage beef, and make tragic plans to barbeque the crazy fucker. It rains like they said it was going to. You retire indoors with a stoopid English smile on your face and your sausage is reciting from *Hamlet*. Look, I don't want to run about in white shorts like an Australian and say to every bloke I meet, 'See you around,' like we all live on a beach or something. But I would like the English people to stop me on the street and say 'It's a bit sunny, if you know what I mean?' God, it's so fucking sad. Not to have language for better weather.

I'm telling you I spray aerosols (flea spray) up at the ozone and chant in Hindi, learned from Raj in exchange for teaching him the meaning of the word 'mad'. Raj says if me and Girl ever achieve a car he will strip it down for us free. Practise for his mechanic course. The only thing I love about England is Raj. I can't stand his father's shop where I have to buy my aspirins and skimmed milk, but Raj is good value. He has given me a piece of his mind free of charge. Respects my analytical skills. Even seeks them out. We have had many a breakthrough in the Pickled Newt. Raj buys me shandy and pretends it's lager because he wants my best attention. Wants me to be sober and serious and I oblige, keeping an eye on my watch. Take the white boys who hid razor blades in the lid of his school desk. Raj wants to pulp 'em on the tarmac when he gets his first Jag. I say, 'Look, Raj, those razor blades are still inside your head. You got to take 'em out and slit your lousy dog's throat with 'em.' He's got the grace to attempt a laugh (I know all about having to simulate mirth from the Grand-Dad episode) but he insists his mom likes to have the dog in the shop for protection. Even though the dog once chewed her knees under the sari. Five stitches and a tetanus. She needs another dog to protect her from this dog.

England is a nation of dogs. When the monarchy goes, it will be a republic of dogs. The Dog Coast. The United Church of Dog. Dog Mansions. The Dog Café. Dog University. Don't know why the bulldog is supposed to represent my country. Frankly I would prefer a gonk. At least I could back-comb its blue hair, put it in curlers and tease it up with a bit of lacquer. A French pleat. A quiff. Gonk ponytails. Gonk plaits. Gonkery. Yep, I've coined a new word for the British people. The Gonkery Dental Practice. The British School of Gonkery. BA Hons in Gonkery specialising in a variety of hairstyles.

Look, my dad bashed me and no one cried except Girl and Mom. No one's demonstrating outside Boots the Chemist from the Billy Rights Organisation, are they? There are citizens out there who would rather cry over dogs than me. Why? Cos dogs can't talk back. They can't say, Fuck off, you fat cunt, you know I hate meaty chunks. Back to the weather.

If the rain stops you get a weird flash of courage and hope. You think you will find a park to read the newspaper in, like they did in the early nineteenth century. Giggling when they fell off their penny farthings. You shiver under a tree whilst reading the paper (particularly the weather reports) because you want to believe this is a pleasurable experience. To believe this simple task has made you happy and emotionally stable. When you stand up you find you've been sitting in a pile of dog shit. Your new suede shoes are fucked. You stink. You're damp. Your hands are shaking cos it's cold. Your newspaper is the only thing you've got with you to wipe the dog shit off your chain-store clothes. You walk home staring at the sky with crazed, betrayed eyes. I want ozone to open wide and zap me with all it's got. Cook me, hotness. Take my weedy little body and tan it. Give my white-boy face an unhealthy flush. C'mon, Big O! Gentle over the biceps and then pulp 'em. I can take it.

Yeah. Things are a bit rainy if you know what I mean. Mom. I dreamt her skin was dry. And I dreamt she died. Two glossy purring animals lie on her bed, surrounded by exotic plants with browning leaves. Under the Xmas tree are some presents wrapped up for her children. Mine is a chocolate stretch limousine. Girl hasn't got anything in hers. It's just wrapping paper. Sometimes I torment Girl, say hers is a chocolate minicab with three wheels. I am very sad about Mom's absence in my dream. I remember her taking calcium pills to strengthen her bones. Painting her toenails. Teasing up her hair for her famous beehive style with a special comb. Sitting with her baby girl on her lap watching the weather on TV. I remember her perfume. It was called Moth. All I know is that moths smell blue. Like the night. I remember sweet complicity with Mom in cafés. She ate a full English breakfast and dunked her toast in the yolk for me.

*   *   *

54

It's a bit rainy, if you know what I mean. Bitter filthy wet fucking rain. No. It's not funny. All that scrambling to shelter under the shitty striped awnings of butcher shops. The giant turkey drumsticks piled up and covered in clingfilm. Blue and goose-pimpled. It's raining. The sweating Dublin chops on special offer just about to pass their sell-by date in a big way. The sticky thick blood of livers and kidneys on silver trays, the second-rate eggs laid out on the counter, the pale rubbery slabs of Cheddar, the bundles of lard dripping in their wax wrappers – and it's *still* raining. The clambering onto buses full of the insane mumbling upstairs and mothers screaming at their kids and fathers who've lost their kids cos they just haven't been up to it and all the sad city dwellers queuing for fried chicken in crappy fast-food chain stores and hardware shops selling mops that don't work to women who can't afford them. Women with broken zips. Mom preferred buttons, like me.

This is not the Wonderland I've been put on earth for. The men in phone boxes with a suitcase between their legs. The boxes of strawberries with all the rotten ones at the bottom. The newsagents with tit mags crammed on the top shelf and little jars of instant coffee and bottles of bleach and lottery tickets and packets of stale factory biscuits.

It won't do. It's not worth having lungs to take breath for. It's not worth waking up for. It's not worth having the vote for. Just one big fucking spectacle of pain.

I remember Mom putting conditioner in her hair and combing it through to the ends. She was always complaining about split ends on account of all the teasing she had to do. Mom had the highest hair in the road. Planting sunflowers that never grew. Bending over to tuck me in. Trying to whistle but it never came out right. It can't when you shop with the pain of thrift in your bones. Mouth. Eyes.

Soon we can have anything we want because we are going to *do* FreezerWorld with the help of Louise and her retard rage. I will be a citizen with big shopping potential, hmming along with the Muzak. Makes the shopper contemplative. Assists the shopper with his thorts. Here's one. Nearly there. Thort coming up.

What's the point of England?

There ain't no empire or industry – not that I want to be a coal slave, as Girl would say, nor do I want to work in a gas showroom – I've seen through it and thru it. Mom wouldn't have liked that for me. Naaa. She wouldn't have liked to think of her clever boy on the shop floor twitching so she has to wash my clothes every day. I don't want wages to starve in a civilized fashion: SPECIAL OFFER: 500 CHICKEN WINGLETS FOR £2.99 – THEY DIED TO FEED THE WORKING POOR. Unless you're just a high income chickaholic and can't get enough of chicken in the form of winglets. Just crazee for the winglet experience, BUSTING FOR A WINGLET graffitied on all the toilet doors – Citizen Winglet fought a short but victorious war in order to defend his lifestyle. Battery birds. I earned 'em.

Billy the beastie in his English lair. The only self-defence is to lie on the straw and get introspective. Go into your self. Snuffle your head deep inside the straw and yawn till you feel strong enough to yawn again. To build something for yourself in your lonely wasted mind, put on a hard hat and enter the architecture on the lookout for wonder. In comparison with that adventure, does Billy want to ride a tank and conquer Haiti or what's left of Russia?

Come off it. I'm not losing a drop of Billy blood for the nobs. Got enough to do, thanks. Fanks. What's the point of England? There ain't the weather like I've discussed with you in an easy-going manner. The only way Billy the beast is going to crawl out of his pain lair is for a snack. I, Billy, fifteen years old, prime cut of English beef, a sirloin amongst boys and boyz, no fat on this lean dude kitted out in his grotty underpants – waist twenty-six inches and that's only if I stick my stomach oot. Ooot for England.

Dad bashed me. That's all. After he bashed me, something happened. But it's gone. Gone to gonkery. Mom set fire to Dad and then she disappeared. Walked through the enchanted garden and out the other side. The wild heath where winds howl and owls shriek. Mom, in the form of her soul, has disappeared into me. I must take maternal care of Girl and make her better.

English pain has opened up a whole crack in the world for me. Cleanse me with swabs of cotton wool, please. Yeah. I'm ready for California. Ready to lie flat out on the blond American sand and become spiritual. Improve my inner being. Like chin implants to improve my profile. 'S long as I never have to wear a baseball cap the wrong way round. Better off with a little plastic chicken winglet around my neck on a chain.

11

'You don't know how to make a margarita?'

Billy and Girl are sitting perched on the chrome and plastic stools at the bar of the Holiday Inn. Girl sulks in shades with striped zebra-patterned frames. Billy wears a herringbone suit. Always dress smart when you're about to rob a superstore.

'You don't know how to make a margarita?' Girl repeats in disbelief.

The barman shakes his head. 'Never had cause to make 'em here. Folk want a gin and tonic, or a scotch usually.'

'Jesus fucking Christ!' Girl is getting hysterical. 'You don't make cocktails in this hotel?'

'Nope.'

'What's the point of him?' Girl shouts at Billy, who just shakes his head incredulously.

'Look, do you know what a cocktail is?'

The barman nods wearily. 'Yep. It's mixers.'

'Jeeezus! Where are you from?'

'Devon, madam.'

'Yeah, well.' Girl looks at him sorrowfully through her new shades. 'Suppose you only drink milk in Devon. *Milk*!'

'Is there something else I can get you, madam?'

'Cocktails are martinis and gimlets, manhattans and margaritas. Martinis have been drunk for *ever*. It's not like cocktails are a new thing! Everyone loves a drink shaken up. You should have a juicer behind the bar for starters and a briefcase busting with bartending tools inside it! You need a bar spoon, a blender, a jigger, measuring cup, mixing glass, paring knife, standard shaker and a strainer. Got any of those things, Mr Barman?'

'I have some lemon slices, madam, if you would like a gin and tonic?'

'Lemon slices?' Girl is amazed and disgusted. She looks at the ceiling and shakes her head tragically. 'You telling me that if I want a garnish for my cocktail all you can offer me is a lemon slice? Got any celery? Cinnamon sticks? Pickled jalapeño peppers? Almond syrup? You think tonic is a mixer? Got any coconut cream? Clamato juice? Guava nectar? Bitter lemon soda?'

'Nope.'

'Okay, I'll tell you what.' Girl lowers her voice and winks at him, giving him a chance. 'If you can't make a margarita, mix me a Mermaid's Song instead.'

The barman looks nervous. 'I can give you a martini, madam.'

Girl stares at him coldly. 'We want a margarita. Have you got Triple Sec?'

'I've got Cointreau.'

Muzak leaks out of the speakers.

'Okay. Have you got tequila?'

'Nope. Not much call for it, madam.'

'Not much call for it! Did you hear that, Billy? This is a bar, isn't it? Have I got this wrong? Is this *not* a bar? Am I wrong about this? Am I in a dry cleaner's? Am I asking the dry cleaner for a margarita and he is telling me there's not much call for it or am I in a bar where you ask for things like a margarita and it is perfectly *normal*?'

'I'll have a beer,' Billy says to the barman, who is backing away now, busying himself washing glasses in boiling water, scalding his hands, trying to remember if his horoscope said today was going to be a good day.

'And don't fucking give it to me in a hot glass.'

Girl bangs her hand on the fake-marble tabletop. Adjusts her new sun shades. Runs her fingers through her blond fringe. Twitchy.

'Billy, it's easy. So damn easy I don't know why we didn't do it years before. FreezerWorld. It's like this, Billy – are you listening?'

'Yep.' Her brother knows exactly what she's going to say. They've already planned it four times. It's been well discussed. They're having a cocktail and then they're going to *do* FreezerWorld. Except Girl is losing it. Taking her nerves out on the barman.

'Sooner we get out of this country, the better. I'm telling you, Billy, this is the last straw. England is *fucked*. I was really looking forward to a margarita.'

When the barman brings Billy his beer, Girl asks for a triple vodka and lime on the rocks.

'I honestly feel like crying, Billy. I was just so excited at the thought of enjoying a margarita. It's too much to take disappointments about small things. It's the *big* things supposed to crack you up, but this is too much.'

'Don't cry,' Billy says. 'For fuck's sake, don't cry!' He gulps down his beer. 'We'll torch the place one day. Any time we ask for onions with our burger and they don't do onions, we'll torch that place as well. Any time we ask for avocado and prawns and they give us pink cream, we'll torch that place too.'

Girl takes off her shades to watch all the more closely as the barman pours lime cordial into her vodka.

'We'll torch Devon,' she says.

* * *

Billy smirks behind his hand. 'Lucky I put my vest on.'

'Why's that?' Girl slamming her zebra shades over her eyes again.

'Cos we're going to *do* FreezerWorld.'

His sister orders another triple vodka.

'Louise. *Louise*, Billy. It's a sign. It's a sign under superstore neon. For us. LOUISE. Louise works on the Cash Only till for *us*. A real princess, big blue eyes and a gold hair slide in her gold hair. She's only been on the tills a week and she hates it. The lights make her eyes hurt. The manager treats her like a retard. She wants to do the store damage, Billy. It's called retard rage! She doesn't know it but she does! That's the most important thing. She doesn't know she wants to help us, but she does. Very much so.'

Billy wonders if she's got a temperature because her cheeks are flushed, the red creeping into her nose and ears. And Girl is a pale girl.

'Remember, her tea break is only fifteen minutes. We got to work quickly. Get it right. Not fuck up. What does Louise do for her fifteen minutes, Billy? She eats an apple. She combs her lovely gold hair. She puts cream on her hands. She takes a deep breath and walks back to the till. That is fifteen precious minutes in the life of Louise. At four o'clock the Saturday girl takes over from her. The till is busting with cash. The supervisor empties it at four-thirty. I'll take over from her at five to four, Billy, understand?'

Her brother nods. Let her get it out of her system. Run through the plan again. Just hope she remembers to take her shades off and not have a Mom catastrophe at an awkward moment.

Girl takes out a checked overall from a plastic bag, FREEZERWORLD emblazoned on its side. 'Louise gave it to me, Billy! I didn't even ask for it. I saw it rolled up by the side of the till. Louise said, "It's my spare. You can have it if you like." She's working with us, Billy.'

She holds up the overall. 'Louise and I have got the same slave garment. Girl slaves wear 'em all over the world. The Saturday *Girl* – get it, Billy? That's me. We're all set up, Billy boy.'

'For fuck's sake, Girl, you're making me nervous. Keep your voice down. Jeezus. The barman already knows exactly where we're going and what we're going to do. Why don't you run it through again with a friendly constable just to clear your mind?'

Girl takes off her shades and lowers her voice. 'Okay. Tell me once more what *you* are going to do?'

'I'm gonna create a disturbance in the store. The staff gather to help me. You're filling a FreezerWorld bag full of cash and you'll just walk it.' Her brother smiles. 'It's so crazy. Sooo crazy.' He whistles.

Girl crunches the ice from her vodka nerve molotov.

'Another thing, Billy. Are you listening?'

'No.'

'When I checked out the shopping last time, there was an announcement. If ever there was a sign burning for us, it was this one: "We want our customers to feel that FreezerWorld belongs to them."'

'Let's take 'em up on the offer.' Billy leans towards the barman. 'I know this is a glass. I'm not asking you to agree with me. I'm asking you to fill it up.'

'Be with you in a moment, sir.'

'Why does FreezerWorld sell garden furniture?'

'How should I know?'

'If something's called CatWorld you don't expect to find parrots and goldfish there, do you?'

'God, you're driving me crazy.' Girl's lips are cold and wet.

'You're already crazy,' Billy says.

'Even crazier. For God's sake, Billy, have a chaser with your beer. We've got a lot on our plate this afternoon.' She takes a delicate sip of her vodka. 'I'm just off to change into my Saturday slave-girl overalls.'

12

'Good afternoon, all newcomers to FreezerWorld. Take your time. Explore our world at your own pace. Here are some suggestions to help you find your way around. All dairy products are on Aisle Three. Right next to our very own bakery. Aisle Three, bake-eree. Say that little rhyme to yourself and next time you'll remember it. Now I have an announcement from one of our FreezerWorld staff. I have just been handed a slip of paper and I'm trying to read the writing . . . yes, here goes. "Who ever stole my Walkman from my locker? I know who you are, signed Mister X. Chicken winglet shift." See folks, we hide nothing from you here. There are no secrets in FreezerWorld because FreezerWorld is also God's world.'

Girl walks to the aisle that sells Ethnic Foods (Eccles and oatcakes) so she can get a better look at Louise. There's a long queue by her Express till. Shoppers with baskets, not trolleys. Louise is floating products over the computer with her limp white hands. Bleep. Bleep bleep. Louise is lost in the land of bleep. Louise *is* bleep. Louise is Domestos and frozen lamb cutlets and frozen onion rings. Her hands and hair are Angel Delight and Cup-a-Soup. She takes money and starts all over again. Retard rage. Girl feels Louise's heat whack into her cheeks. It's twenty to four.

A challenge for the FreezerWorld community. How do you get the new plant of the month home in the family car? A yucca. A *big* fucking yucca. A whole forest of them out in the car park. Spilt earth everywhere. A customer crushing the leaves of her plant in her rush to get to Express before the man with the heaped basket of nothing but taco shells and jars of salsa sauce.

Girl does not dare to catch Louise's eye yet. Better to come back at five to four and begin the long walk towards the toy section. Killing time. The toy section is of particular interest on account of her being called Girl right up to her seventeenth year. Girl dolls with the bodies of young women.

All the girl princesses. Standing proud in the FreezerWorld toy section.

White girl princesses, of course, they always are – froth of see-thru gauze and little gold shoes. Boxes of white plastic girls. The special FreezerWorld brand of princesses, like the special FreezerWorld brand of pork rashers. Princesses of the Frozen World, sneering at Girl with their tiny lips, lips for snowflakes and rice grains . . . little mouths always open in an O, ooooo, standing in their golden shoes inside their boxes, right next to the crisp shelves.

Snax. Smilers, squares, twirls, rings, salt 'n' shake, munchies. Girl is exploding into crisp packets and they are exploding into her. Cheese-and-onion-flavoured shards needling into Girl flesh, double crunch, sour cream with chives, dying into the scampi fries, freaked out by the new-flavour Stilton-wedge crinkle chips.

The princesses with their big hair. Luned-out stares. Blue-eyed devils. Tiny lips, oooooo lips.

Whath yr name?

Girl.

Girl? Thath a funny name. Heee heeee.

Squeethe me and I say, Go away, Girl frm Hell. Polluting me with yr hideouth soul. You're a sicko if I evr saw one.

Girl strokes the doll-princess hair through cellophane. The

princess in her lovely garden, painted on the box. Doves and butterflies and old-fashioned roses.

Go play in the other section. You don't belong here.

You donth belog here.

Where is it I don't belong? What kingdom am I banished from? I want to touch the doves and I want to press rose petals in my diary.

Go away. Go find anuuther toy. The one with the lickle horns and fork with pwongs. The one with the warths and the bwig nose. The one with the fwangs and pointy eerths.

Girl says, Listen, cocksucker. Don't do your segregation thing on me. I am you. I am a Girl princess and one day I will have a kingdom too. I will be in love and ride in taxis, kissing my prince. We'll stop at restaurants that look like they're going to give us a good time. The waiters will buzz around me in my blue minidress with the see-thru heart. My prince will have eyes only for me. I will be full of enchantment. Enchantment twinkles inside me, unlike you, squeaker. You are dead. Someone made you dead. That's why you have to be squeeeeezed. Don't talk of your own free will cos you're dead. Someone deaded you. In a princess factory. You talk other people's words. Talk white trash. Talk white bread. Talk margarine. Talk pinkie-ring talk.

Princess changes her tune: Let's be friends, Girl. I love you. I'm only a virus anyway. Squeezed into Girl bloodstream for ever. I'm contagious matter transmitting princess infection into Girl. A corruption. A pathogenic agent. A combination of chemicals increasing rapidly inside living cells. Girl cells. Got no vitamins inside me: vita meaning life. Do something, don't just stand there staring at the snacks.

Snax. Girl is fainting into the crisp shelves again. Chilli garlic. Salsa with mesquite, four cheeses, tomato and basil. *Dhansak puri* fading into chilli and lime tortilla, T-bone-steak-flavour

66

crinkle something, pastrami bagel aaaaaaaar pain something forging its way into Girl's body. Pain something opening its eyes and mouth. Tingling terrible something, invisible, insidious, making its entrance in the superstore light. Aaaaaaaaaaar. Citizen Pain. Astronaut Pain standing on the moon, pain walking because there is Mom. If it isn't the princess, it's Mom.

Drunk. Head bowed over the frozen sweetcorn. Aisle Three. Mom's fate is girl's fate. Mom is girl's internal crucifix. There she is. Mom lives in FreezerWorld. Citizen Frozen. FreezerWorld is the only world that will have her. Concentrate on the potato snacks. Snax. Tomato and sweet pepper four cheeses treat prawn cracker salt 'n' vinegar. That *is* Mom with her kind, bleary eyes and worst worst worst of all, Mom is holding the little pink shoe in her hand, the left little shoe, one of a pair, Girl having nailed the right shoe to a piece of wood to keep for ever. Move to the juice.

Move to juice quick. Where is Billy? Juice. Look at the cartons and give whole Girl self to them: Five Alive, five fruit burst, apricot and guava, mango and passion fruit, aaaaaaaaaaaaaaar, orange 'n' passion fruit, cranberry with vit C, raspberry 'n' apple, strawberry crush. Mom 'n' Girl.

Five to four.

Louise looks cute in her overalls, her blond hair tied back, hands scrubbed. The Express till is the most popular queue in FreezerWorld. Customers are only supposed to have six items in their baskets. Basket people are rebels and refuseniks. Cheats. They load up as much stuff as they can and Louise doesn't care. She just takes their cash and hardly ever looks up. Girl walks right up to the till.

'Tea break.'

Louise nods, head still bent, but her blue eyes flicker for one second towards Girl's hair. The roots are coming through the blond.

'Okay,' she says, 'I'll just finish this lot. Funny sort of Express this is.'

A basket person is packing five frozen ducks and twenty boxes of frozen garlic bread into FreezerWorld bags.

Louise says, 'You press this button here to open the till, and this one to close it. Cash only.'

'Right.' Girl makes faraway eyes like the information is not important.

Louise is persistent. 'Don't take cheques or cards. They sometimes try to trick you –' she points to the queue – 'they pretend they haven't seen the Cash Only sign. Some of them load up three baskets and still come to Express. They're cunning. Do anything not to queue with the trolleys.'

'Cash only,' Girl says with feeling.

''Nother thing.' Louise stands up and moves out of the way for Girl. 'Sometimes the till's stiff. Won't open. You have to call Mr Tens.'

'Right-o.'

Louise takes a lipstick out of her overall pocket, squints while she smears it on her lips, glances at her watch and walks off.

Girl reaches for whatever is nearest her hand. A packet of chocolate-chip cookies. Bleep. Seven more packets of chocolate-chip cookies. Five tins of meatballs in tomato and basil sauce. Jeeezuz. How do they cram them into the baskets? Girl wants them to shove the whole of FreezerWorld into their baskets. Two bags of nappies. One large tin of powdered milk formula. Three bleeps. One tiny weeny tin of spaghetti rings. Two jars of rollmop herrings. The herrings won't bleep. Nothing happening. No red light, no green light.

Complete fucking silence. It's like there's been a nuclear accident and there's a horrible calm in FreezerWorld. A rustle in the undergrowth and then silence again. A big sad sky. A bottle of 4711 Cologne lying in perfect condition in the ash. A mangy teddy bear with one shattered glass eye sitting on a pile of corpses. The world has come to a standstill. The end of FreezerWorld, Girl can't bear it when the silver herrings tremble as she floats the glass over the bleep border. Nothing. The fish hasn't got what it takes to get through. Girl tries again.

The customer has an anxious expression on her face. Girl hates that look. She hates it particularly because her first customer is one of her Mom-check specimens. The one with gonk slippers and tissues. The Mom with the Polish husband. Herrings for her husband. Jeezus. What bad luck! Can't get away from them. FreezerWorld is probably crowded with mother material. Didn't she just see her real mom on Aisle Three? Girl punches numbers into the till like she went to supermarket school at five years old. She lets the herrings go. Get that woman out of her sight. Go. Back to Poland with your husband and die in a tram crash.

Girl tells herself: If something doesn't bleep, let it go. Thing is, she wants the money. It's like she's management. If it doesn't bleep, ring it up, punch numbers in, any numbers. Get cash. A basket person waits with basket fear in his heart. Two bags of frozen prawns. Two bags of steak chips. Two trays of pork rashers. Two tubs of peanut-cluster ice cream. Two pots of noodles. Two potatoes. Whaaat? Two potatoes? Why is everything in twos?

Aaaaaaaaaaar. It's a soft sound. Aaaaaaaar. The breath trickles out of her lips. Pain inside Girl. Crackling inside her Girl form.

69

The shoes. The little pink shoes. They come in pairs. Girl has one shoe and Mom has the other.

Twelve giant economy bags of lo-calorie crisps. Girl looks up from bleep. The customer is a woman, that's the important thing. Fat white arms. Lo Calorie. Kwik Bake. Rol and Bake. Every single woman in FreezerWorld could be Mom. Girl wants to interview every one of them. She presses the Open button and the till drawer slides out effortlessly. It's crammed with cash. Girl handles it like she owns it, counting the notes possessively. A bit resentful about giving change. Like she's giving away something that is hers. Keeping an eye on Billy who has just appeared out of nowhere and whisked the NEXT CUSTOMER PLEASE ruler onto the sliding belt. Girl sneaks a look at the mountain of goods heaped in his trolley. A senior FreezerWorld citizen stares at him in dismay. She could be Mom. Kind but firm. She shakes her head at him and says something about Till Five. Billy looks puzzled and hurt. She points to one of the other tills. Mimes him wheeling his trolley over there, far far away from Express. 'Express is baskets only,' she explains slowly, dragging out the o-n-l-y. He gasps like she's explained the meaning of his presence in a universe where everything is energy and nothing is certain. Baskets only. Thank you so damn much for that information. It's changed Brother Billy's life. Like when he's cycling at night and he hasn't got lights and he's wearing black everything, and a kind motorist takes time off to point out that he, Billy, has not got lights. If only he had known. Thank you for that insight. He'll walk his bike the twelve miles home now and ruminate on the information; so dense and perplexing is it, he won't even notice the blisters on his feet, the muggers, the drunks, the runaway kids in their sleeping bags, the night rats chewing winglets and suet and Valium, the kerb-crawler blokes with their lack of hair and toilet-chain bracelets, or even the rain so cosy with its pitter-patter. So much to think about and so much time to think it in. Billy plunges his arms deep into his trolley. Yep, here it is. A giant-sized Frozen Family pizza: JUST LIKE MAMA USED TO MAKE. He flings it onto the sliding belt and walks his trolley to the other side of the store.

Girl glances at her watch. Give him thirty seconds.

Bleep. Bleeeep. Bleeep. Music to Girl's ears. Where is FreezerWorld Louise? She's due back any minute.

Three uniformed FreezerWorld staff (little black bow ties) are running through the gleaming aisles. They are like paramedics, moving in unison, running and talking at the same time, revving up to crash through the emergency swing doors of superstore surgery. Bruising past soporific shoppers wheeling their trolleys in a trolley ballet, reaching for bread and biscuits and cereals and teabags. Someone shouts 'He's bleeding, call Mr Tens!'

Bleep.

Girl thinks, Billy is okay. But not that okay. The till is working like a dream. A crowd of customers are gathering near the Toiletries section. Billy's weedy voice gabbles something about the razor blades not being properly wrapped. Girl turns to the queue by her till. 'Move to Till Five, please,' she insists in a Don't Fuck with Me voice. Customers look at her in numb disbelief. It is as if she has just told them a relative has died. Girl fixes them with her most malevolent stare.

'This till is out of order.'

No one moves. Girl points vaguely to Till Five.

'Over *there*. This one is *not* working.' Jeezus. If she had a gun she'd mow them down. Haven't they got homes to go back to? Children and lovers and pets waiting for them? Appointments to keep? Customers. Dazed and confused. Jeeeeezus. Get on with it. Get a life. But this is the Life. FreezerWorld life. Is there life after FreezerWorld life?

At last. At *last* the queue begins to disperse, but not without mutterings and complaints about how they deliberately chose a basket and not a trolley even though a trolley was easier for them and how they would have shopped differently if they had known they were going to have to queue in the trolley section. Some of them, Girl is informed, might as well shop all over again because if they are going to have to queue with trolleys they might as well do a week's shop instead of just a weekend shop. What's the point of just popping into FreezerWorld to get one item on special offer if they have to wait behind those customers doing a family shop, an extended family shop by the look of that trolley over there, and anyway, just take a look at where Till Five is – right over the other side of the store. Management should provide a courtesy shuttle.

Girl is pressing the Open button and the till is stuck. It won't budge. And it's making a strange bleeping noise, a new kind of bleep with a different tone. A red light is flashing. Not only that but some grotty customer with ginger eyes, God, how do you get to have *ginger* eyes, is asking if Girl knows which aisle does green washing-up liquid? Girl, preoccupied but still playing sweet, says, 'They're all green,' but the customer has turned into a citizen and he's muttering on about ecological washing-up liquid. Girl sends him to the diabetic jam section. One last punch of the fucking Open button. Nothing happening. She's going to have to do a runner, empty-handed. She might as well kill herself there and then. What the hell did Billy do to ooze out all that damn blood? Cut himself with the lickle knife he saves for cinema seats or what?

How does she kill this new damn bleep siren? Press everything. Press every button in every combination. More staff are running over to where Billy is. Someone has turned the Muzak up. Is Billy alive? Did he slit his throat? A young black man saunters over to the Toiletries aisle carrying a bucket and mop. Jeezus. Hope he doesn't get Billy blood on his trainers. That would really be a lousy way to end the day. Yes Yes Yes Yes. The till is open. Girl takes a FreezerWorld carrier bag and begins to pack wads of notes into it, fast but calm, looking around but no one's looking at her. The basket people haven't even reached Till Five yet.

Till Five is Terminal South compared to Terminal North. It's colder in that part of the store. They speak another language there, Trolleyspeak. It'll take a bit of time adapting to the new culture. Never mind, Basket People. Learn the ways of the Trolley People. Join in their feast days. Get used to their humour. Enjoy their music. Understand their superstitions. Watch out for diarrhoea and dysentery. Comply with Trolley bureaucracy, red tape and visas. Become familiar with tipping procedures, toilets, time zones, opening hours and water. Finally, Basket People, avoid blood transfusions unless absolutely necessary and always wear a condom.

Saturday Girl is working fast. Go for the fifty-pound notes first, then the twenties, forget the fives, might have time for the tens.

The PA makes an announcement: 'Mr Tens. Mr Tens, please come to Till Five. Mr Tens. Mr Tens, please come to Till Five.' Might have time for the tens. A nice wad of fifties. Thicker than Girl's thighs. 'Mr Tens, Mr Tens, please come to Till Five.' Billy's voice is drowning under the PA. He's shouting about how he's going to sue the store for damaging his hand and he wants to see the manager. He wants to see Mr Tens. Mr Tens is the most wanted man in FreezerWorld. Everyone wants Mr Tens except Girl. She wants the tenners, small potatoes but she wants them after all and she is just about ready to go. Mr Tens is making his way through Aisle Three. Mr Tens.

FreezerWorld superstar. So much gas in Mr Tens, he's got a bigger bow tie than the rest of the male staff and he's got a different pace. Girl presses the Close button. It slides like a perfect cremation.

Mr Tens looks a bit anxious. What's wrong, Mr Tens? Will your children inherit a better FreezerWorld than this one?

Girl slips off the chair and moves over to pick up the pizza. She puts it in her FreezerWorld bag with the cash, walks out of the store into the car park and takes off her overalls.

Time to smoke a gold band menthol. Smoke and walk. Walk fast, smoke like there's all the time in the world. Smoke like she's on vacation wondering which beach taverna to drag herself to next.

FreezerWorld really is a good world because Girl has just caught sight of a Freephone to order a cab. What perfection. Girl is truly grateful. A cab will arrive in five mins, enough time for another menthol and to comb her hair, which is stuck to her scalp with warm salty nerve sweat.

Jeeezus!

Girl doesn't know what to do. She has just seen Louise.

On the other side of the car park. The dark side. Louise is not on her own. She's saying something. Her lips are moving. She's not fully dressed, or rather, her dress is hitched up to her armpits. 'I gotta go, Danny, I gotta go.' Danny's got his hands everywhere on anything to do with Louise. His jeans are undone, his face buried in Louise, lifting her up, putting her down, lifting her up, her arms wrapped tight round his neck, laughing and fighting at the same time. And then something terrible happens. Louise looks Girl straight in the eye. Her lips are moving. Her eyes poking into Girl's eyes. Louise says, 'I'll be seeing you later.' Girl knows the words are for her. When the cab splutters into the car park, she dives inside quick. Sweating.

Louise with Danny the prince. Denim round his ankles. Danny the dog prince. Doing it in the car park with Louise. Girl can feel a great girlhowl coming on, making its way west through her body.

Weather warning. Stay in your homes. Board up your windows. Switch off all electrical appliances. Call in the cats and dogs. Bring your pet rabbits and tortoises inside. Stop your washing machine mid-programme. Those of you unfortunate enough to be out walking, find a church and lock the door. Even the cab driver well used to motoring barely human life forms to their destinations – even he who is surprised not to be abused by his passengers – jumps in his seat when Girl asks him to stop outside Oddbins and wait.

Wait while she buys a bottle of tequila, a bottle of Triple Sec and a pack of menthols. When she climbs back into the car, cursing Billy out loud for not thinking to get lemons and limes instead of goddamn pizza, the driver is surprised to find himself checking that his radio phone is still working. Sometimes it just blanks out and he can't get directions when he's lost. Yesterday he spent two hours trying to find Trafalgar Square. Eventually a Japanese tourist gave him detailed instructions and even then it was a long haul. No wonder the ashtray is overflowing with butts and foul squibs of spat-out chewing gum with teethmarks in it.

Girl throws a FreezerWorld tenner into his lap. When she slams the cab door, the window falls out, completely intact, and drops six foot into the hole where the road is being dug up. Girl checks for one terrible second that she hasn't left her FreezerWorld carrier in Oddbins, though she knows she hasn't because she's just parted with some of her precious bleep loot. She just stands there in a daze, watching the driver roll his trousers up and climb deeper and deeper into the hole. Look at that fucking car. Someone should show it the way to the cab cemetery. Her pulse has gone crazy. She's going to be sick and then she's going to make a margarita.

The driver grips the glass under his arm and clambers out of the hole. When he finally manages to open the boot, a complicated task achieved with a screwdriver and a two-pence piece, he wedges the glass between a vital part of the engine that fell off yesterday and an exhaust pipe swapped that very morning for a windscreen wiper.

A tenner! That sobbing psycho didn't even ask how much the ride was. What's wrong with girls these days? Even his seven-year-old daughter has started to get stroppy about him practising his three-point turns when he takes her to school in the mornings.

Whining, but never looking up from her book on quarks.

13

Weirdness in Billy's face. Slow freaked paces across the kitchen lino. Billy is home. Ho-me! Bandage wrapped tight round his hand from casualty, clutching a bouquet of flowers, compliments of FreezerWorld, in his good hand.

'Five stitches. Blood everywhere.'

'God, Billy! What you want to cut yourself like that for?'

Girl sits him down, lights him a menthol cigarette and gives him a glass. 'Best margarita you'll ever taste, Billy boy.'

Billy takes a gulp, punches his head, sends the whites of his eyes up to the ceiling, pokes out his tongue, rises on tiptoe, spreads out his arms and throws himself against the wall.

Mom and Dad are masked dancing figures on stilts. The sun is shining well into the night, damaging concrete and skin structures. Birds stalk their prey on suburban lawns. Billy has his ear to the ground. He is a catastrophe theorist who will export his mind like grapefruits and potatoes to every corner of the globe. But for now it's gone quiet. Panic quiet. Girl inhaling exhaling menthol. Billy hallucinating scenes of macabre margarita beauty. Mom in a tiara made from ice. Dad waistdeep in snow caught in a storm of bees. Images for his first book on pain. Pain is as mysterious as love. A world of feeling and silence. Mood changes and sobbing. Both enter the body, love and pain often the same thing. Both cause profound change and even death. Biographies, symptoms, histories.

'Could have done with a few days in the hospital.' Billy eventually staggers up from the floor. 'A lovely nurse bringing me my cup of tea in the morning. Time for the doctor's round. Morning, Billy England. And how are we feeling today?'

'Start packing, Billy. We're off.'

Her brother walks to the oven and turns the gas down to four. 'Pizza's burning. Gas too high. Always read the instructions on the box.'

'There's a cab coming in one hour'.

Billy doesn't want to hear departure words. He is somewhere else already. Can't be in two places at the same time. Pain is a place. Too heavy-hearted to be a tourist.

'There was some commotion on Till Five. All the baskets fighting it out with the trolleys. Tens is chief of the FreezerWorld tribe. But he just can't work out what's happening. He can't control his own people. Doesn't understand what makes 'em tick. There was one man who only had a loaf of sliced bread in his basket. He went mad. Totally cracked up in Trolleyland.' Billy's whining morose voice.

'I mean, there is Tens being mobbed by the Basket tribe. Does he reach for a couple of bottles of FreezerWorld champagne? Give them a complimentary drink? No. He offers to give the basket people an IOU for any special offers sold out while they were on the long march to Trolleyland!'

Girl opens the oven and takes out the sizzling four cheeses pizza just like Mama used to make.

'I said, there's a cab coming.'

Not just a bit rainy. It's bucketing down, if you know what I mean.

*　　*　　*

78

'I did a Mom check in FreezerWorld.'

Girl has gone quiet. Sinister, Billy thinks while he shovels the pizza into his mouth. Not quiet, downright sinister.

'She was holding a little pink baby shoe.'

Billy waves his bandaged hand to stop her talking, but Girl's voice is hardly there. Her eyes are shutting down. Over and out. Mom is like the phantom limb of an amputee. It tingles in the stump where she once was. Pain is not just in the body. It is in the mind and soul. Call Himmler. Call Dr Ruth and Oprah. Call Oscar Wilde and Descartes. Most importantly, call FreezerWorld Louise. Anyone who knows a bit about hurting.

'Naaaaaa.' Billy is fading too. Screwing up his eyes like he's gone snow blind. 'Those shoes were a free gift. A FreezerWorld promotion. They all had one. Every single Frozen customer had one. They got bubble bath in 'em.'

Billy knows his sister is about to cry her girl tears. Got to keep talking. Talk all the way through grief and out the other side. Thing is, all words have stopped. He wants to go to bed. He hasn't got any summer clothes to pack. On account of the weather. Got winter clothes. Clothes for the cold. Trying to talk sunshine and shades but all words have stopped. Ice in his mouth. Shivering. Wants animal skins and furs. Girl has taken out the cash and is counting it at the table, tears pelting onto the fifty-pound notes.

'Louise said she was going to see me later.'

'Yeah.' That's the only word Billy wants to ever say again. Not too much effort. Yeah.

'She's dangerous.'

'Yeah.'

'Know what she does in her tea break?'

'Yeah?'

'Does it in the car park with Danny. D-a-n-n-y.' Girl puts as much disgust into her voice as she can.

'Louise helped us, Billy. She doesn't know she wanted to, but she helped us all the same.'

Her brother puts his arms around her thin shoulders. 'You're a heroine, Girl. You were brilliant.'

'Louise wants us to save her. From Mr Tens. From Danny. From the Frozen World.'

Billy takes notes in his head. Girl is his patient and Girl is his sister. When he is famous and the TV cameras travel across his pain features and make them a public spectacle, he will say, 'Take your time. Stare at me without embarrassment. Don't feel you have to look away. The great pain tundra of Billy England. I will wait if you have to inhale from your asthma machines. I will wait if you have to telephone your families to say you will be late. I will wait while you order coffees and Danish pastries from your subsidised cafeteria. I will even wait while you snort cocaine in the toilets.'

'It's a respectable cash haul, Billy.' Girl is whispering now. Big smile. Big enough to cross the Thames and not fall in. 'It's enough. Run me a bath. The last bath I will ever have in England.'

Part Two

1

Billy and Girl thought they were heading for California. Knew all about America from the brochures and TV. Imagined themselves drinking daiquiris under the palm trees and blue movie skies. 'Cept it wasn't the big buck agents, the surf and Disney pets that wanted them. No Mickey and his lovely first lady Minnie in her lickle white gloves to welcome Billy and Girl to the land of plentiful. No TexMex was to pass their lips. No tax-free shopping in Tijuana. No healthy walks through miles of mall to stretch the legs and get blood circulating pronto to the remaining shards of Billy and Girl heart-hacked with English weather problems. No Florida crocs and beauty-queen mermaids to tickle their pain history and stretch lips into knowing kitsch smiles. Girl was never to become a Nevada cowgirl sprayed into denim and photographed for gentlemen's leisure mags. She thought she would be wearing high-cut orange bathers and shooshing her peroxide fluffy hair when she spoke to male lifeguards all muscle and morality and mega-hormone narratives. Poor Girl. I mean, can you see her scrawny white-bread English thighs lazing with the Californian beach girls? English Girl with her introspection and minicab rage and no cosmetic surgery to armour her and no sweet talk inside her to simper its way out and get involved with local boyfriend and beach-life issues? Girl buying donuts in bulk to bait every obese woman she meets into giving her an interview? Hi, Mom. Have a donut. Have three. No. That's all over.

*   *   *

Billy was not to be discovered by Hollywood highballs on Malibu beach in his Speedo minitrunks. Not that kind of boy icon. For a start, even with a tan, even with a personal trainer in a deluxe Malibu gym, Billy is not reliable or predictable. He can't be trusted to learn his lines. Writer delivers script. Director reckons this is the one to swipe all the Oscars on the big night and he is already getting his wife to write his speech. She's faxing a draft to him right now. How he discovered William The English singing 'Twinkle, twinkle little star' whilst strumming a toy plastic banjo, and how he just knew, with Great Director's Instinct, that the boy was a screen God for the contemporary world. Billy is wined and dined, groomed and flattered. Billy eats with gusto. Bloody steaks flap off the sides of his plate. Fistfuls of Californian french fries are shovelled into his boy mouth. Billy never has to eat another chicken winglet again. He gets a little plumper but won't do arm curls, not even with the starter weights that even a poodle can lift effortlessly with one manicured pawkin. He reads the script. Agrees to be a star. He'll play a sulky James Dean reincarnation called Jonnie. His co-star is an apple-pie babe with attitude and her character is called Candy. They go over the script together and then the big day arrives. Billy has to be dragged kicking and screaming out of his trailer and pushed onto the set. The scene is set in a moody bar.

JONNIE: See you're drinking beer.
CANDY: Yeah. So what?
JONNIE: That's a good brand.
CANDY: I know.
JONNIE: Mind if I sit here?
Candy shrugs. Jonnie sits.
JONNIE: I feel really good sitting next to you.
CANDY: (*Secretly flattered*) Well, thank you.

Not too demanding, is it, Billy? Lights. Sound. Action.

BILLY: See you're drinking beer?
CANDY: Yeah, so what?
BILLY: That's a good brand.
CANDY: I know.
BILLY: Mind if I sit here?
Candy shrugs. Billy sits.
BILLY: You remind me of my sister.
CANDY: *(Improvising for camera)* Oh.
BILLY: She won't let me fall in love with other girls.
CANDY: Is that right?
BILLY: I don't mind. Cos I'm frigid.
CANDY: *(Catching director's eye. He's saying busk it.)* Uh-huh.
BILLY: Completely totally fucking frigid.
CANDY: *(Cracking up now)* We'll soon do something about that, Jonnie.
BILLY: Frigid.
DIRECTOR: *Cut cut cut cut!*

Okay. The English boy has a kind of anti-charisma that's interesting. Inneresting. Let him ad lib. Look at him. He's taking out a little pen knife and cleaning his fingernails. That's not in the script either. Okay. *Okay.* But hang on. Frigid? *Frigid???* Can't have boy icon say he's fuckin' frigid. Not good for box office. Not good for the plot. Not good for the next scene when he has to take Candy home and make love to her in the shower. Cos the only power Jonnie's got in this movie is his bad-boy sex appeal. So why not give Billy England a chance and try shooting that shower scene? See how that goes and then come back to the bar. Okay. So

Candy's in the shower. Jonnie's got to take off his kit, climb in with her and soap her breasts, real slow and sexy. Thing is, Billy The English won't take off his clothes. No matter director and art director saying he can keep his pants on. This boy doesn't even wear short sleeves. No way. Says in England he showers in his anorak. That's why it's waterproof. Director thinks, Let's get a little experimental. Why not? We're ahead of schedule. Let him.

Lights. Sound. Action.

Billy English fully clothed gets into the shower with naked Candy. He takes the soap. What does he do? Starts washing his fucking hair. Standing under shower in anorak washing his hair. Inneresting. Only thing is he's got lines scripted for him by the writer who is sobbing into his script, shouting something about never working again. Never let the writer near the shoot. Big mistake. Jonnie is supposed to say, 'I've been wanting to do this ever since I first saw you in the bar.' Do what? Wash his hair while naked nubile looks on? I mean, what kind of pervy movie is this?

So now actress playing Candy is going berserk. Wants to call her agent. Says why don't she wear her skis in the shower? Hell, why not eat a Caesar salad in the shower? Director gets an idea. He's not giving up on Billy England. Says to Candy, 'Okay, sweetheart, tell you what. Talk dirty to Jonnie while he soaps his hair in his anorak.'

Okay. Camera's rolling. Candy narrows her eyes. Voice honey low. 'Hey, Jonnie. I want you to do things to me.' She presses her breasts against his anorak. What does Billy do? Billy screams. Got soap in his eyes, hasn't he?

Director turns to camera. Genuine disbelief. Gestures to Billy. Someone take him away. Hang him. Mince him into mad Heritage British beef patties and feed him to the welfare single mothers and their bastard brats.

Billy informs director that he's got a pricking pain all over his nerve fibres. He's not quite sure where the site of his injury is but he's researching the whole phenomenon and it's his life's work. All he knows is that pain is a black box full of mystery and one day he will unpack it for the reading public. The boy feels he has to explain further. The whole crew gather round. Make-up, continuity, gaffers, all-purpose electricians, the extras playing pool in the makeshift bar, the runners and boom-swinger guy who seems to be in some sort of shock because his arm is frozen in midair and he's muttering something about an aeroplane overhead when he's not even recording. Every time his eyes graze those of Billy The English, he shuts them tight so he doesn't have to put a face to the whining voice cracking into his head, wasting his time, encouraging the director to go berserk and sack the whole crew while he recasts.

Billy is saying, See, it's a chronic interdependent kind of pain, a union of what the Greeks call the psyche (mind) and soma (body). He, Billy England, is perfectly aware that he is addicted to his pain. It is his narcotic, and he must give it up and endure cold turkey etc., but before he can do this he will have to find a way of declaring his grief before he can reshape it. Finally, Billy gasps breathlessly, finding an opportune moment to reach for a smoked-salmon bagel from the catering staff, is the director familiar with Freud's description of cancer of the jaw being like a 'small island of pain in a sea of indifference'? No? Well, he, Billy, is the small island of English pain in the Hollywood Hills, could someone pass him another bagel pleeeese? No, not salad. No, not egg mayonnaise. Billy England is a neurosurgeon of the mind – he will build stone cities, carve into rocks, build railroads of the mind, but for now his own soul-tissue damage precludes the possibility of being a boy star.

When the director's jaw actually drops open, culled into silence by this gobbling goofy goy guy ranting in his wet anorak, Billy can see the thousands of dollars of dental work that have been put into the famous director's teeth and gums. Billy wants that kind of attention too. Not in the dental department, though. No. Billy is not reliable. Girl knows this. Look how he nearly sawed through his wrist to create a small diversion in FreezerWorld? Billy. Gulp.

Billy and Girl are Mom-and-Dad pain bonkers. FreezerWorld lucre. They counted their stolen loot again. Minicabs came and went through the night. Girl has some distant memory of being Empress of Minicab Empire. But the infrastructure had gone. Bombed itself into oblivion. Call another cab. She punched in the numbers, dazed and shivering. Practising her big smile. Wiping it off again. Arranging words in some kind of order, not knowing what they meant. Bad-tempered drivers banged on the door and left cursing without a fare. Eventually the minicab office banned all calls from number 24 Harkham Road. Billy and Girl can't even drag themselves to bed, never mind into an aeroplane full of potential Mom-check material.

Counting the notes, skipping numbers to avoid the catastrophe of counting in sequence. Girl saying, 'It's a respectable cash haul, Billy.' Big smile on. Big smile off. 'It's a respectable cash haul, Billy.' On. Off. Billy waving his bandaged arm, whining. Wanting haddock. Moaning for haddock. *Haddock?* What the fuck is haddock? It's a fish, isn't it? Is it? Nothing is certain any more. California? You grind it with glass, don't you? Chat shows? That's one of seventeen words for snow, isn't it? The doorbell ringing. Another aborted cab. Counting the money over and over.

Six hundred pounds.

*   *   *

Not exactly a mega robbery. Not exactly. If they're lucky, it's two cheap fares from a bucket shop. Plane diverted via nine destinations, having to endure the company of cheery sunseekers spilling airline boeuf stroganoff over their hideous T-shirts. Girl dressed in her Jackie Onassis outfit. Shades and a little red suit with white trimming. No tights, just her silver loafers. Complaining bitterly to the stewardesses about the lack of cocktail know-how. Doing her nut when she asks for a Bloody Mary and the air hostess hands her a miniature Smirnoff and a can of tomato juice. Screaming for real service. Demanding half a teaspoonful of horseradish, Tabasco sauce and a lime wedge in her fucking Bloody Mary. Billy howling, biting the cushions when she changes her mind and insists on a Bosom Caresser. Five parts brandy, two parts Madeira, etc. Girl might look like Jackie and Billy does his best to act presidential, but they're not exactly set up for idle luxury once they arrive in California, are they? Only Grand-Dad's envelope of cash, and that's not predictable if he hasn't had much luck on the horses. No. Unless they luck out and get spotted immediately? Like at the airport, showing their visas to immigration. A Pain Agent behind them. Her big blond hair gleaming with the latest monkey-gland sheen spray. Yards of fingernails painted orange. Tapping them against her perfect teeth. Sussing them out. Converting their English pain potential into US dollars. Pain Agent's best catch yet! Whispering into her mobile. 'Al, I jus' hauled in the biggest tuna the Golden State's ever clapped eyes on. Buy a new freezer, I'm draggin 'em home.' Not exactly.

Six hundred miserable English pounds.

    FreezerWorld let them down. The Basket People let them down. Louise let them down. The Express till to nowhere. A robbery to nowhere.

*   *   *

The morning after, Girl cleaned the skirting boards and Billy swept the kitchen floor. Billy scrunched up newspaper, soaked it in meths and scrubbed every window in the house. Girl washed down the sofa, armchair and curtains. Billy collected every odd sock he ever owned and rinsed them in biological. Girl took all her bras out of the drawer and soaked them in bleach. Billy undid his bandage and gawped at his stitches. Girl trimmed her fringe and then burnt the blond ends in an ashtray. Neither of them answered the telephone. The answermachine whirled and clicked and the voice droned on and on. Always the same voice. Girl rubbed suntan oil into her cheeks and lay on the carpet reading a thriller. Billy sliced one mushroom for ninety minutes. Girl washed the suntan oil off her cheeks. Billy put his bandage back on. Six hours and four messages later, Girl pressed the Play button. Yes. Definitely the same voice on all the messages. Girl searched for Pause, and then she called Billy. As soon as he saw his sister's face he knew he shouldn't have rushed slicing that mushroom. Sat himself down on the most comfy armchair, crossed his legs, fiddled with the laces on his red trainers, asked his sister whether she wanted to rub more suntan oil into her face before she pressed Play? No, but she has just spotted a speck of dust on the woodwork and would he mind if she takes a moment to dampen a J Cloth and remove it? Of course not. And while she's in the kitchen looking for the J Cloths, would she be so kind as to put a lid on the dish with the sliced mushroom inside it? With pleasure. In fact, she'll clean out the fridge while she's there to make room for the dish with the mushroom in it. Perhaps while she's doing that, Billy could take the gold bands off the butts in the ashtray and save them to make a Christmas card with? What a good idea. Why doesn't he make a little box to save the gold bands in?

Girl presses Play. The same message, four times. Dad's voice in their front room. Speaking to them. Dad leaving a message for his kiddies.

2

THIS IS A MESSAGE FOR WILLIAM AND LOUISE ENGLAND.
I THINK YOU MIGHT BE INTERESTED IN A CAR I HAVE TO
SELL YOU. MY PHONE NUMBER IS 0115 676767.

WILLIAM AND LOUISE, I CALLED EARLIER WITH A CONTACT
NUMBER. I KEENLY ADVISE YOU TO TELEPHONE ME.

YES, I WOULD LIKE TO SPEAK TO BILLY AND LOUISE. MY
NUMBER IS 0115 676767.

BILLY AND GIRL. THIS WON'T BE MY LAST MESSAGE.
AS I SAID, I HAVE A CAR YOU MIGHT LIKE. I HAVE REASON
TO BELIEVE YOU HAVE SOME MONEY TO BUY IT WITH.

'Call him, Girl.'

Billy's gone blue like he does when he's painwalking. Trailing his mind across a landscape of soft ash. It's warm where he is. Warm and chalky. White birds hover above, flapping their wings, making wind for the ash to rise and scatter.

Billy is naked. Rolling in the ash. A small boy. Face down, rolling over and over, blue skin covered in ash, like talcum powder, fifteen years old, perfect and tiny. Rolling the pain out of his baby fifteen-year boy body, fifteen summers and winters.

'I can't.' Girl punches her blond head, eyes shut, lips shut.

'We must.' Billy is nearly home from his walk. The blue is leaking out of his face. He takes a breath, wants to sound weary and assured. 'We must. I'll tell you why.'

'Why?'

'Mom.'

'He doesn't know where she is.'

'He might.'

'I can't.'

'I will then.'

Billy stands up. Walks to the telephone. Cradles it under his chin. 0115 676767. Waits. Thinks about all the mushrooms in the world that need to be sliced. His sister can see the blue creeping back into his fingers. Painwalking again. Someone's interrupted his stroll. Up to his waist in ash. Saying something.

'Hello. This is William.'

Pause.

'When?'

'Ten o'clock?'

Pause.

'Ten o'clock.'

Billy puts down the phone. The important thing is not to look at Girl. Look at the telephone cord instead.

Girl says, 'What happened in the pauses, Billy?'

Billy counting every whirl in the spiral of white cord. It could be the intestine of a small animal. Something that scampers in the woods and hides in trees.

'Dad says he saw an artist's impression of us in the papers. Wants to reassure us it isn't very good. Nothing like us. But he's our daddy and dads know.'

Girl cheers up. 'Oh, really? An artist has done a drawing? That's fantastic, Billy! We're famous! I wonder who described us to the artist? Some basket person, I reckon. Probably the one with the ginger eyes. He saw us in *ginger*!'

Billy wants to give the plastic cord a little saucer of milk. Anything to distract himself from the terror scraping at his throat. Terror to do with Girl.

'Thing to do,' he begins, pushing down the fear coming at him from somewhere forgotten, 'is to go and see a film now.'

'Yeah.' Girl nods.

'Cos we got to leave for Nottingham early tomorrow.'

'Yeah.' Girl nods again, freaking her brother out.

'We got to be there by ten o'clock.' Billy knows he's got to leave the room. *Now.* He's beginning to tremble. Not because of Dad. Because of Girl. Because of what Dad told him about Girl in the pauses.

'Pass me my menthols, Billy. I think I'll have a smoke and think about Dad.'

Billy needs to take a walk. There's no way he really wants to see a film with his sister. It scares him the way she's sitting there, drawing on her cigarette, smiling to herself. 'Thinking about Dad.' He puts on his coat, suprised to find his feet pressing extra soft on the carpet, moving stealthily towards the front door. Closing it in slow motion so as not to disturb Louise. Taking a breath hurts his boy mouth. He's never called Girl Louise. So why is she suddenly Louise? Why everything? Dad called Girl Louise. Please please make it Raj's day on.

Billy opens the door of Patel's English and Continental Groceries with dread in his heart. What if Mr Patel is at the till today? Raj's father treats him like a kid. No respect for his analytical skills. Last time Billy told Mr Patel he 'was in denial' (Mr Patel was laughing over something Billy thought was extremely sad), the old man doubled up with hysterical laughter and suggested Billy take up judo at the local sports centre. Today Billy doesn't feel up to the Mr Patel treatment.

He doesn't want to be given a complimentary mini choc bar. The old man feels sorry for him. Jeezus. Doesn't Patel know he's been straightening out his son this past year?

It's Raj all right. Billy can hear the stress in his voice. Trying to take the money for a packet of Quavers that a prominent member of Stupid Club is reading.

'Anything else, George?'

'But then again, Raj, I had an uncle who was a scientist and he said take no notice of the sell-by date.'

'Yip.'

'He said if it smells off, don't eat it. If it smells right, who cares if it's a month past the date?'

'Yeah. Bye.' Raj looks in desperation at Billy, pleading with him to do something.

Billy obliges. 'Fuck off, Professor. Closing time.'

George's mouth quivers. He turns to Raj. 'Want me to punch him, son?'

'No, George. I'll set the dog on him. See you tomorrow.'

At last. At fucking last Stupid Club George fucks off out of the fucking shop.

'Fancy a half, Billy?'

'A *pint*, Raj.'

Raj raises his eyebrow. Never seen Billy like this before. In fact, his pal looks like he's swimming in the insanity lane. Worst of all, he's playing with a little mushroom. Keeps transferring it from one palm to the other, like he's thinking something through. Raj tries to keep an open mind. Okay, so what's the big deal about using vegetables in unpredictable ways? Why not carry a carrot in your pocket for luck? Why not hang a broccoli floret around your neck to ward off the evil eye? He takes out a packet of bacon from the fridge and throws it to the Alsatian, who catches it between his sharp crusted fangs. Dog saliva dribbling down his mangy black gums. Raj switches off the lights and locks up the shop.

'Good boy. Don't forget to say your pork prayers.'

3

'What's up then?'

Raj is patient. Just sits there drinking his third pint of strongest draught lager, waiting for when Billy's ready.

Billy strokes his mushroom with the ball of his thumb and then shuts his eyes. For a long time. Three pints' worth of time.

'Did you know that Girl's real name is Louise?'

'That's a lovely name.' Raj smiles. 'Suits her.'

'What would you say, Raj, if I told you that Louise set fire to my dad?'

He's still got his eyes shut.

'Set fire to him?'

'That's what I said. Burned up his face so he had to have a new one grafted on. The skin from his chest put on his face.'

Raj is feeling dizzy. It really has been a hard day. Truth is, he feels like sobbing into a cash 'n' carry Kleenex. What with Stupid Club George and now Billy with his fire stories, Raj can't walk. He staggers to the bar and orders another pint and a half. Zigzags back spilling beer on the carpet.

'Why did she do that then?'

'Cos Dad tried to kill me.'

Raj suddenly wants to go home. To sit at the kitchen table and eat a tasty chicken curry. Drink a mug of milky tea. Watch TV with his father and little brother and ask his mum what she wants for Christmas. In fact Raj bursts into tears. Lays his head on the table and sobs, cheek pressed into a beer mat.

'It's all right, Raj. Was a long time ago.'

Raj shakes his head, searching for words to slur and slide into each other. Drunk. Bloody legless. 'I just can't take any more of Stupid Club.'

Billy chucks his mushroom under the table. It's an effort to open his eyes, it really is.

'Listen, Raj. You're the best thing England's got. Don't give up hope.'

Raj lifts up his head and vomits over the table.

Billy just can't believe how unhelpful his pal is being. He's going to have to carry him out of the pub. Billy, who's not supposed to be there in the first place. Billy, who only comes up to Raj's belt buckle. Stupid Club are really doing Raj damage. Cos what they do, Billy reckons, is dump their collective pain on Raj, in the shape of Quaver and sell-by-date talk. Look at him. That's what comes of being an unpaid pain counsellor. What a day. Billy stands up, grabs hold of Raj's arm and flings it over his weedy shoulder. Starts to drag him across the balding carpet, past the jukebox, past the builders staring at him with cement in their nostrils.

Outside in the cold, Raj sobers up, loosens his shirt buttons and wipes his mouth.

'If your dad tried to kill you, then Girl saved your life.'

'Maybe.' Billy's turning blue again. 'I don't think she remembers what she did.'

'Probably a good thing.'

Blueness sliding into Billy's cheeks. He looks tiny out in the fresh air. Shrinking or something. He's beginning to look like a plastic toy in a cereal packet.

'You all right?'

'No, I'm definitely not all right, Raj. Do I look like someone who's all right?'

'No.'

'See, Raj, I don't want to be anywhere near Girl when she remembers.'

4

Girl

Dad didn't look like Dad. He came to the door and we didn't know who he was. Dad used to be the best-looking prince in the kingdom. He had a new face. God must have zapped him. Stretched his arm through the sky and lightning bolts exploded from his fingertips onto Dad's head.

His eyes were small. Dad had *big* eyes. This Dad had a face sewn on. Lips too near his nose. Slime dripping from his ears. This Dad had no hair. Smiling with his wrong lips. Staring with his wrong eyes. Staring but not looking. This Dad was shrunken. Shrunken but not small. His eyes kept poking at us. First Billy. Little jabs. Then me. Staring but not looking.

Billy said something about how we've come to the wrong house. This Dad shakes his wrong head. 'No. You've come to the right house,' he says. Dad's voice. Deep. A prince's voice.

It was the voice that got to me. The same as the answermachine voice. Dad's looking at me from out of his ears. I told you his face is put on the wrong way. I say, 'I don't want to come in.'

He nods. 'Didn't think you would.'

Billy says, 'Show us the car then.'

This Dad stinks of beer. This Dad's voice is coming out of his fingers. He's starting to walk. One two. One two. We're following him. Dad in front, his kiddies behind. My father.

Takes half an hour opening a garage. Tries five different keys. Perhaps his fingers don't work properly? When he got burnt he must have put his fingers over his face.

Staring but not seeing. Staring at his son's tattoo with Mother on it. Beckons us inside. It's dark in the garage. We don't want to go in. Dad stands there calling us. He stinks of paraffin and beer. We're not budging. Just standing while he calls us. Calling us with a different name each time. William. Louise. Bill. Lou. Billy. Girl.

'Well, you come on your own then, lad.'

Lad? Billy is rooted to the fucking concrete. Lad? Dad might just as well have said Tin. Even without the 'lad' bit he'd never go near Dadness. Last time he got too near he wound up with a broken arm. As far as Billy is concerned LAD = BROKEN ARM. We all had to draw hearts with a Biro on his plaster-of-paris sling.

This Dad shrugs. Just calling out versions of our names. 'Bill, Lou-Lou, Will, Girl.' Changes his mind and gets into the car himself. Starts the engine. Nothing happens. Tries again. Nothing happens.

Billy says something in my ear. Stupid stuff like we shouldn't buy a car that doesn't start. Oh, is that right? Billy should edit an automobile journal with inside knowledge like that. The car-owning public really need him. So I whisper the sad facts into my brother's ear. 'We got no choice. He's blackmailing us.' Just as Dad manages to start the car and backs it out onto the street. Don't get too excited. Once upon a time it was a car. A Merc, 1959. Would make a lovely minicab.

Dadness is getting out of the Merc wreck like a car-crash survivor. I don't know what he's thinking because his face is probably somewhere else on his body. I might be looking at his arse for all I know. 'Thought you might like this,' he whimpers. But his voice is teasing us. Teasing and whimpering.

What does Billy do? He looks at this Dadness, trying to figure out where he begins or ends, and says, 'Where's Mom?'

A complete fucking pig-squealing silence. Dad is going to disintegrate and restructure himself in front of our eyes. He's going to melt down and shape into something worse. This Dad says, 'Mom had to disappear, didn't she?'

What does Billy do? Boy detective? Deadpan voice. 'What have you done with Mom?' Jeezus. This Dad has probably eaten her. He's going to burst out of his skin and splatter the Merc with slime.

'Took the blame, didn't she?'

Stop Dad talking. Saying things. Better to buy the Merc and go.

'After Louise burnt me up. Mom said it was her who did it, didn't she?'

Take out the cash. Take out the cash. Take out the cash.

How much does he want? This Dadness with his beerness. Paraffin stink. His made-from-something-elseness. 'You owe me all you got.'

Something smashing my head with a stone. The things that girls owe. What do I owe Dad? He's looking down at his feet so I can see the sores on his head.

'We didn't make much.'

This Dad nods. 'Yeah. I know. I read about it in the papers. About six hundred quid. I'll have that.'

Whass happening? How did Dad know? What's he been saying? Just his wrong lips moving. Let's get *out* of here.

Dad's nostrils watch me take the cash out of the bag. 'I've got to go now,' he teases and whines. 'Buy a few cans before the off-licence closes.' He holds out his hand.

* * *

I used to walk hand in hand with my father. Down stairs. Up stairs. To the shops. He used to put his hands over my eyes and lift them off and he used to take me swimming. I used to swim towards his hands. Waiting there. To catch me. Dad hid things in his hands. A mint chocolate or a mini-Christmas-tree teddy bear. Choose which one to open. Always something there for me in Dad's hands.

When I put the money in his hand, he grabs my hand. Hard. 'Tell me where Mom is, pleeese, Dad?'

Something happening to Dad. Tears leak out of his small wrong eyes. Spring out sideways. Like a water leak in a tap. 'It's not what happened to your mother you should be asking,' he gulps. 'It's what happened to your father.' The tears are seeping from under his skin. Wetness springing from the sides of his lips. Pouring out of him. He won't let my hand go. He won't stop saying things. Stop. Stop. Stop. Let go of me. Stop. Stop it. Stop saying. Stop doing my hand. Stop. Just stop. Stop. Stop. Let go of me. 'My Girl, girl girl girl,' he whimpers and leaks. 'My girl girl girl my girl my girl girl girl girl my girl my girl my girl girl my girl my girl.'

5

Billy

Mein fader. My first ever sighting of manliness. He came to
the door knowing his kiddies stood on the other side. Dad last
saw me when I was ten. I shave now. Shave the cat that is.
Heh heh heh. Look, I'm a man of science. It's my career, tho
no one knows yet the extent of my influence. I am a fledgling
founding Leadre of Twenty-Firdt Cntury Thought. Thort. But
I have to confess my teenage sighting of Dad sent me primal.
Whirling through the caveboy vortex into fire, fat and flint.
Demon terror. I nearly let Christ into my life. On the verge
of turning my palms upwards and inviting all the dogs in
England to come unto me. Pedigrees and mongrels. Nearly
prayed for golf programmes to be on *all* the TV channels *all*
the time. Then I got a grip.

Dad is good-looking. Always has been.
   Girl hid her face in her arm when he came to the door.
When Dad's blue movie-star eyes roved my boyness I saw
exactly what Mom must have seen in him. I'm going to faint
because Dad is a sex god. How did such a big man get to have
a runt of a son like me? Dad has been well and truly punished.
Not that he stood in front of us in repentance. He stood there
in defiance and drunken mean plotting to get his kiddies' stolen
loot. Righting an injustice against him. Righting his blood sugar
level with Special Brew. Six hundred quid's worth.

Dad is an old-fashioned Dadness. There won't be many more of him in the future. Not when I publish my book. A new sort of Dadness will be born. After the first crucial five minutes, it was all right for me, meeting Dad. I understand the situation. I tried to steal Mom from Dad. Baby Oedipus. Oedipussy. Mom's disappearance is my punishment for cheating on Dad. The equivalent of gouging my eyes out with a brooch pin. A flood of gore, 'black rain' running down my face, staining my beard. If I had a beard.

I knew what I was doing when I wooed Mom away from Dad for ever. Call on me any time for definitions, explanations and concepts. I'm a major boy theorist. The Neeetcher of Harkham Road. Yeah, if anyone ever bought me a gonk I'd call it Nietzsche. I can't understand why I'm not a hunchback or something because according to my books, there is good evidence to suggest that unresolved emotional stress will always find a way of afflicting the body. I might be small but I got no wrenches or twists. A perfect little tragic boy pain icon.

So what if Dad tried to mince me into Billy burgers?

'S long as I don't seriously think this is the one and only way of doing Dadness, I'm all right, aren't I? The books say so. I mean, you would trust me with your pets when you go on your holidays, wouldn't you?

My sister tried to make Dad invisible at first sighting. You know how she did that? Naaaaa. No magic fucking spells or curses or walking in a circle three times. She shut her eyes. Louise. Girl. A menthol spook. When she opened her eyes she made them go retarded. To Let. Vacant property. Unfurnished. Poked her fingers into her cheeks. No crying yet but I had mentally prepared myself with even sadder thoughts: like Raj selling raffle tickets to send himself to college. I promise to tell the truth. There is nothing sadder than Dad and Girl.

It's a love affair. I could see love in the vapours between them.

Girl set fire to Dad on my behalf and Mom took the blame. That's how the story goes. Why did Girl want to destroy the person she most loved? That was the terror when I first heard. What I am saying is, I hope I am not the person Girl most loves. Dad is the prince of the twentieth century for Girl. I, Billy, will be the new brand of prince for the twenty-first. Even if Girl had tried to kiss him better, this frog Dad, nothing would have happened. What could Dad have changed into? The world has changed and he needs a new story. But no one ever told it to him. What if my sister *had* kissed frog Dad and a prince had popped out? The old story prince, from another time, another age. What's his equipment? A sword. A white stallion. A wedding ring. A castle somewhere? What's the modern girl princess gonna do with that stuff? She wants her own equipment. A good sound system, two credit cards and a stash of Ecstasy for the weekend. And her own gonk.

As it happens, Dad's stallion was a fucking beat-up Merc. Worse than the minicabs Girl keeps in business. Dodgy protection, like I said before. The prince Dadness didn't even know the words of the *old* story. Hop onto my stallion and I'll lead you to a better life. He sold his fucking knacker's-yard stallion to his kiddies. And then he cried. Hollered. Clutching princess Girl's hand. Putting the car keys into her hand for danger money. Girl who can't drive. Now I know where Girl gets the crying gene from. I really thought Dad was going to cry himself into the atom structure. Into the concrete. Cry himself into the brick walls and tarmac and old fridges and cookers lying around the place. Lou Lou Lou Louise. Saying it over and over like it was a magic spell. Jeeezus. Get my sister a Ramos Fizz immediately. Six parts gin etc. But don't get her loving me *too* much.

I've hardened up. Scholars have to. It's not ideal to experience pathos and terror first hand. We must push on into the future, cry over better stuff than this. So I just asked Him the only thing I want: Where's Mom, where's Mom, where's Mom? And Dad mutters something about how he hasn't got the words. You know what? He's right. He hasn't got the words. You'd think tragedy would teach us about ourselves and the world. Well, it's taught Dad fucking nothing. He has no tragic vision, no stature of any kind. Future Dad will have the words. He'll have the equipment. The feelings. He will be All There. Cos otherwise he's just frog Dadness, and there's a shortage of princess girls to kiss him better. A regular famine of princess material. Heh heh heh. I've suffered for my insights.

But my time has come. Once I've sorted out this Mom thing, nothing will stop my manliness walking proud in the twenty-first. Yep. I'm gonna walk tall with Raj. Cos Raj is the best thing England's got going for it. And Raj's moment has come. Via the Merc.

Frog Dad disappears into his house. Probably eating slime and flies while his kiddies check out their pain-family inheritance. Neither of us have a clue how to drive it home. Girl turns the key and what do you know? It starts first time.

Now what? We don't even know what thing is clutch, what is accl and what is brake. Not for one moment are we going to ask frog death. Girl turns off the noble engine while I make a call to Raj. I'm standing in the phone box at the end of the road, begging him to catch the train up to Notts and save us. He's saying there's no one to look after the shop.

'Raj, close the shop. You'll love this Merc. It's beauty and truth, Raj! So damn big you could fit the whole of your dad's shop inside it. Drive us home, will you? Look, Raj,' I scream, 'if we see the whiteboyz who stuck blades in your school desk, we'll pulp 'em like you said you wanted to, okay?'

Raj isn't falling for that one. I've done too much work on him. It's the Merc that gets him. I offer him one-third ownership if he drives us home.

It's dark by the time Raj arrives. Girl's going nuts because we can't even kill time with a cocktail. Frog father doesn't live in cocktail land. Too much time on our hands. Saviour Raj. Speechless when he sees the Merc. Can't believe he's travelled all this way to part-own something stuck together with frogspit.

Girl is on best behaviour. Gives him a little kiss on his ear. So he gets into the driver's seat, Girl in the front with him, I'm in the back. We all take a deep breath, Girl chanting mantra for a Frozen Matador, four parts tequila etc., and the fucking automobile starts, no problem. First time. Raj cheers up a bit. Puts his foot down with a bit of ownership pride. Jeezus. Frog Dad even gave us a full tank! Girl's relaxing now. Stretches out her legs, sneaks secret glances at Raj. Never seen her do that. Raj is showing her how to do the business. The gears, clutch, handbrake, mirror. Apparently you have to look in the mirror a lot. I can do that. And then, just as it's all going so well, the Merc shudders and cuts out. Girl and I were expecting it, of course. Our pain inheritance wasn't going to be four seven eleven I'm in heaven, was it? So we're all out in the cold while Raj is mending stuff, swearing about what a pile of shit this wreck is, how it's going to take him a year to strip it gown and get it on the road. Nowhere to even buy a Cornish pasty. I mean, what's the point of England if you can't even buy a Cornish pasty in the Midlands? I'm telling Raj how he's the brother I never had and Raj is telling me how much he's going to charge me for the new parts he's going to have to buy. Girl's smoking one menthol after another, trying to get frog-prince grief out of her head. Raj is lying right under the Merc disaster now. I'm promising him a Billy pizza experience when we get back home.. That gets Girl screaming so loud the rear light falls off. Raj stands up, groaning. Instructs Girl to mend the light with the tape in his toolkit. Miming with his fingers, round and round. Raj watches her, hands on his snake hips. Runs his fingers through his hair. 'Girl and Billy England,' he mutters, 'the whole family is *fucked*.' Girl smiles. Next thing I know, she's in the driving seat, and Raj is sitting next to her. I'm lonesome in the back and Girl's driving as if she was born with a car key in her mouth.

6

Girl hopes the Merc is going to change her life. The days
of minicab protection are over! She watches Raj remake the
Merc with real excitement about all the rides they're going to
go on, a thermos of margaritas in the hamper. She sits on the
bonnet, Raj under the car, just chatting. Telling him about
her life view and what she thinks about certain events. He
loves mending the Merc. Makes a change from selling dead
fruit to Stupid Club.

Because Raj is always under the car trying to figure out how
to fix something that was made in 1959, he doesn't get to do
much of the talking. Anyone walking past the Merc would
think Girl was sitting on the bonnet talking to herself.

'I hate it when people say, Are you all right? What are you
supposed to reply? You fall over in the street, rip your elbows
and scab your knees. Someone comes over and says, Are you
all right?'

Raj smiles under the car. Even though she can't see him,
maybe she can feel his smile? He's also noticed that she's
wearing blue knickers with a little flower pattern on 'em.

'You're hurting and just want to bawl. Everyone watching
and your bag's tipped over the pavement. Are you all right?
They know you're not all right, Raj! They *know* that when
they ask you.'

Girl crosses her arms and makes herself comfortable.
Watching a Stupid Club member go into the shop. Probably got wind of the mince pies Raj's father bought in

bulk from the plumber who came to mend his central heating.

'I don't believe in being brave, Raj. I'm sick of courage. When do you have to start with this bravery requirement? Jeeezus! Who wants a row of medals clinking on your Mothercare anorak?'

The truth is Girl and Billy are getting over their exposure to Dadness. Quiet is required. Hot baths. Small activities. Choosing a moisturiser. Cutting up cinema seats. Talking to Raj. Leafing through *Harpers and Queen* to see who has been drinking champagne with who. Sometimes going out to write MOM CALL HOME messages. Whipping up a banana milkshake afterwards. Trying to get to sleep without thinking first. Watching the neighbourhood cats slug out their territory battles.

Raj listening. Enjoying himself. Thinking about Merc parts and the pretty pants Girl wears and how her talking to him makes him feel happy.

All the kids in England. Being brave. Being all right. Being okay.

7

Louise pressed the doorbell at number 24 with the tips of her small fingers. Just a little tinkle. 'Nothing to worry about' was her message.

The lightest of pressure. The smallest of interruptions. When Billy heard it, he wanted to lock himself in the bathroom. Girl said, 'Nothing to worry about, Billy. It's only Louise.'

Louise is not pale. She's past being pale. Girl can see through her cheeks. Louise is wearing a minikilt, leggings and horrible shoes. Shoes with no hope in them. Beige rubber soles.

'Hello.'

Sweet. She's painted clear varnish onto her chewed-up little nails to strengthen them. Somewhere, despite the shoes, Louise cares. The silky blondeness of her hair. Girl reminds herself that she's got two plastic heart hair clips for Louise upstairs. She wants to put them in for her. A middle parting. Clip on each side.

Louise is wearing a bottle-green turtleneck jumper. A jumper with zero attitude in it. Only the tartan mini is any good – just like in Girl's dream. Louise needs to be dressed by an expert. Girl is already going through her own wardrobe making up outfits for her. Louise has got a dimple in her cheek and a vial of asbestos dust in her eyes. The Louise eyes. They grab you just when you think you've got away safe and sound.

Girl is going to play dirty. This is her house after all and

Louise is just an intimate stranger. What the fuck is she doing here?

'All right?'

'Yeah.'

Louise could really be beautiful. Girl is being brave.

'Do you want to come in?'

Louise nods. Of course she does. Girl has known this for some time. The Louise tangle. Louise walks in in her horrible shoes. It's the shoes that hurt Girl most. Louise has arrived. Girl points her in the direction of the kitchen where Billy is making tea. Billy is very busy. The tea takes up all his boy concentration. What with the teabags and the water all having to get to the teapot. That would be a good topic for Stupid Club – the time it takes to make a pot of tea. Girl knows that Billy is working out the meaning of this event for his book, that's why he's so slow.

GOD, Billy! Hurry up. Talk about the weather. Talk about paindogs and how it's a shame milk isn't delivered to the door any more!

Louise takes something out of her bag. Aaah. It's a slab of marble cake! From FreezerWorld. She gets a special staff discount on all items from the bakery.

Really? Billy's making conversation at last. He's seen the cake. Glanced at Louise, close up and from a distance. Conversation! Here it comes!

'Thanks.'

Girl offers Louise a menthol. Louise stares at it for a while and then shakes *no* with her silky hair. She stares at Girl when she lights her cigarette, watching everything Girl does. Billy pours them all a cuppa. Teatime! Tea and cake. At home with the Englands.

Louise's voice is deadpan. Speaking facts. Speaking the truth. 'I've come for my cut.' Little hands reaching for a slice of marble cake. Lips puckering to sip the tea.

Billy's eyes flicker towards Girl, who is sending him an SOS via brother and sister know-how. Shut the fuck up and leave this to her. Girl is still playing dirty.

'You've come for your cut?'

'Yep.'

'Cut of what?'

Another sip of tea. Another little peck into the marble cake. Speaking facts. Watching Girl tap her silver loafers on the kitchen lino. 'Cut from Express.'

Girl's beginning to feel bitter. So Louise thinks the Express till was a big deal, does she? Six hundred miserable fucking pounds. If Louise had got her act together and packed the peas faster, Mr Tens would have promoted her from Express to a full-blown trolley till. More groceries. More cash.

Louise and her horrifying princess eyes. 'I gave a description of you both.' She pauses. 'But I gave it wrong.' The Louise dimple creasing her see-thru cheek. She's flirting a bit with Billy, would you believe? 'They did an artist's something. From what I said.'

'It's called a likeness.' Girl tries to disguise the sneer in her voice.

'Yeah. 'S nothing like you. Or him. Cos they knew it was two.'

Billy is revving up. Licking his lips. Fiddling with the spare button sewn into his shirt sleeve. The manufacturer's precaution against loss. Girl can see what's coming. Billy is going into Dr England mode. Dr England and his talking pain couch. Louise is Billy's patient. Something sensible is lurking in him. It always terrifies Girl when Billy goes sensible. He's rearranging the furniture inside Louise's head. Except the furniture is fucking weird to start with. The table's got no legs to support it in the first place but Dr England is going to move it somewhere. The armchair's got cigarette burn holes all over the seat and Billy is going to shove it against the wall. Rolling up the rug and sweeping up under it. Putting it back in a different place. A whole room of weirdness rearranged. Jeezus. Why doesn't he just chuck out the furniture and leave the room empty?

Billy has been in pain training since he was born. Girl is *so* freaked out by the sense look in Brother Billy. She doesn't much care for being rearranged by a crazy. Just look at him.

Billy puts the tips of his fingers together. They make a flesh cage with a hole in it. His voice is coming through low and clear. A subtitle is passing through his vision like an autocue. LOUISE DESCRIBES RETARD RAGE ON BILLY ENGLAND'S COUCH. Now he's speaking in his new voice. 'Did you help Girl then, Louise?'

Louise seems quite happy to play patient with him. Lifting the table with Dr Crazy, lugging it from one side of the room to another. 'I did help her.' Pointing to Girl, who's blowing menthol smoke all over the marble cake. 'The girl. Her. She's the one who I gave the FreezerWorld overall to.'

'Yes,' Billy agrees with her. 'I know you did, Louise.' Dr Crazy thinks he is being reassuring. Showing her in every way he can that he is there for her. 'Why did you help her?'

Louise scans the marble cake like she's going to pick up her next answer from inside its centre of sugars and E-numbers. Not once looking at Girl.

'She was Action Girl. I knew she would do sumthing. I just think things. I would leave the till and go with Danny. It was timing. Timink.'

Girl stubs out her cigarette. Jeezus. Whatever happened to

Revelation? Whatever happened to the New and Thrilling? She knows all this stuff already. Better help Louise out.

'We know all this, Billy. She's CouchRetard. I'm Action-Retard.'

Her brother looks confused.

'Yeah.' Louise nods enthusiastically. Looks at Girl with admiration in her barmy eyes. 'That's it. What she said.'

Billy's flesh-cage fingers are squishing and opening while the girls speak. He just watches when Louise starts to have a coughing fit. Doesn't even bang her on the back or get her a glass of water.

'Scuze me. Coughin. Coughink. Got to meet Danny in a minute.'

Billy nods. 'Girl said she saw you in the car park with Danny.'

'Yeah. He's my boyfriend.'

Girl is merciless when it comes to Louise doing it in the car park. 'Danny the dog prince. You can do better than that, Louise.'

Louise plays with a gold signet ring on her finger. Dog-prince jewellery. Hers. 'Danny's all right. Coughink again. Sorry. Coughin. Wait. Nearly done. Koughin coffi coughin. Yep. Stopped.'

Girl won't tolerate dog-prince loyalty. 'You need a better make than Danny, don't you, Louise?'

'Danny's all right. Mum likes him.'

Dr Crazy's turn now. Billy England on the case. 'What's all right about him?'

'Does nice Dad things if I ask him to.'

Billy and Girl in brother-sister unison now. 'Like what? *What* sort of things does *Danny* do?'

'Takes me out for a drink. To the fair if I ask him. Pays for all the rides. Mum says he's kind and he is.'

Girl is clutching her split ends now. Grabbing them in her hand, making a ponytail, about to take the knife to them. Look, it's like this: CouchRetard has the same name as *her*. They're both called Louise. If girls called Louise think Dog Prince is the best they can do, then Girl who is also Louise is destined to end up in the arms of dog princes in car parks everywhere. Mongrel princes with their lousy love trinkets and denim jackets.

Louise is annoyed now. There's a reason why she came, isn't there? She wants her cut. Reckons they made off with about six hundred quid. She wants two hundred of it. That's as fair as she can get. Not half. A third. Her share. She wants it *now*.

Girl leaves the kitchen. Let fucking Billy England finish off the session then, he's the one who's supposed to have the certificates in the pain game. She rummages in a drawer in her bedroom. Finds the little pink hair slides she's been saving for Louise. Not only that. Girl checks out her shoe cupboard. Got to give the FreezerWorld girl a better start than beige-sole sadness. Can she bear to part with the orange patent-leather ankle boots she's only worn twice? No. Yes. Yes. She will, because this is an important day. Danny might go off Louise if Louise looks *good*. If Girl dresses her.

She's got to groom Louise. Give her a better attitude, take her out for cocktails. Use up all the Grand-Dad cash if necessary, and it *is* necessary. She's got to rescue her from the Frozen World. Get her smoking expensive tobacco. Make her into a star. Get the retard out of her bloodstream. Even Billy working on her mind can't be a bad thing. Girl has got to create Louise so that she too can become Louise, her secret name. Girl wants to step into a Louise that she has made perfect.

By the time Girl walks back into the kitchen, she can hear her brother putting Louise right. He's telling her the truth.

How Dad read about the robbery to nowhere. Dad rang up. How they hadn't seen him for five years. Dad 'sold' them a car. Dad took all the cash. Dad wouldn't tell them where Mom is. There is *no* cash any more, Louise. Nothing. Just something that was once a car.

Louise looks sad. Really sad. 'I wanted to buy something for Mum.'

That's when Girl comes in. 'I got something for you, Louise.' She hands her the little packet.

'What is it?'

'Open and see.'

'You open it.' Louise gives the packet to Billy, who unwraps the tissue paper with maximum effect, opening his murky pain eyes wide, teasing Louise, hoping Girl hasn't flipped and parcelled up a rabbit's head or something. Just two pink plastic heart hair slides. A sort of Louise/Girl heart transplant. Louise cups them in her hand. 'Oh.'

'Shall I put them in for you?'

Louise is reluctant, seems a bit nervous for the first time. So Girl just takes charge. She will be Louise's beauty therapist. Combs Louise's silky blond hair loving the feel of it in her fingers. Carefully makes a perfect middle parting and clips a heart each side.

'Gorgeous.' Girl is genuinely pleased with herself. Billy is nodding too. Flattering Louise. Louise has got a bit of attitude in her hair: Girl Irony. The hair slides have taken away a bit of retard-rage giveaway in Louise. 'I got some shoes for you too.' Girl shows her the orange ankle boots. A real sacrifice. Saint Girl.

But this time Louise draws the line. 'Naaa. I don't. Naaaa. Danny wouldn't like them.'

'Just try them.'

Girl is on her knees tugging at Louise's beige rubber soles.

Louise has *got* to wear these boots. She has *got* to meet Danny the dog prince in them, cos Dog Prince won't be able to fuck her any more. Cos some of the retard will have gone from Louise.

Girl knows the boots are much too big for Louise's tiny feet but she doesn't care. Louise stands up in them. Walks about the kitchen. She asks to have a proper look in a full-length mirror. They haven't got a full length but they can show her what she looks like in the bathroom mirror. First the hair. Louise is really pleased with the hair slides. Smiles so the dimple shows itself. Pats her hair each side of the parting. Then Billy and Girl heave her up so she can see the boots. Standing either side of her, lifting her high so that her head is touching the bathroom ceiling and she can see her feet in the mirror. No. Naaaa. Look, she doesn't like them. All right, she'll wear them just this once. See what Danny says.

Louise is sweet. Billy and Girl like her. They're going to teach her things. Louise is fucking dangerous. She turns on them in the hallway. 'So you can't give me my share of your cash then?'

When brother and sister agree this is the sad outcome of the robbery, Louise kicks the wall with her new orange boots. 'You'd better give me your dad's address then.'

Billy's up to his neck in pain ash. Girl never wants to talk about Dad again.

'Well, he's got *my* share.'

Billy's come back. 'Yeah, you can have his address.' He takes a purple felt-tip pen out of his pocket. 'Got some paper?'

Louise just rolls up her sleeve. 'Write it on my arm.'

Big letters. Complete fucking silence while he scrawls in unjoined writing, DAD'S ADDRESS, all over Louise's see-thru skin.

'If he doesn't give me *my* share, I'll get Danny to see to him.'

Louise and her spooky see-thru skin. Pink hearts in her hair. Dimple in her cheek. Shiny little nails. Louise is looking good. Tartan minikilt and orange ankle boots. Heavy gold signet ring on her second finger. Looking good apart from the dog-prince jewel. Louise. You can't do anything to her. She's got that look about her that tells you so. Louise. Don't mess about with her. She's a live wire. KEEP OFF THE LOUISE GRASS. NO BALL GAMES HERE. DO NOT ENTER. But Billy has entered. Started with her head and he's not going to stop.

'When you see Dad, ask him where our mom is, would you?'

Louise has a think. 'Yeah?'

'Sweet-talk him. Get him to relax.'

'Yeah?' She's frightening, this Louise girl.

Billy just won't let go. 'Flatter him, you know. Tell him you like his . . . um . . . buttons! Get him in the mood for small talk. And then just slip it in. Where's your wife, Mr England?'

Louise opening her lips a bit now. 'Sounds like you want me to do it with him, Billy?'

Billy is past it. Whatever *it* is, whatever Louise is doing to Billy, he is past it.

'Just get the information, Louise. Whatever you have to do.'

Louise shrugs. Sneaks a little look at Girl. 'Cheerio, then. I'll tell you all about it.'

8

Louise really loves her mother. Most girls prefer their dads because they can flirt with them and get away with more. Not Louise. She flirts with her mother who can't resist her – even though she is extremely worried about her daughter at the moment. For a start, she is perplexed about Louise's new hairstyle.

Mrs O'Reilly is sitting on the couch watching a hospital sitcom. She always cries when someone goes into intensive care and the doctors are huddled round trying to save their lives. She makes herself white-bread sandwiches with the crusts cut off before her programme starts, but doesn't touch them till the credits come up and she knows the outcome. So she doesn't pay Louise much attention when she sits next to her and starts to unlace her new orange ankle boots.

Louise thinks they're fucking hideous things. Danny liked them, though. Stuck two fingers in his mouth and whistled in appreciation. Picked her up, whirled her about and then started to get intimate with her ankles. Sticking out his tongue and licking the orange patent, closing his eyes in a boot swoon. They're not even her boots. Danny likes something that's not her.

Soon as the credits came up, Mrs O'Reilly turns her cheek towards her daughter for a kiss. Then she sees the pink heart hair slides and goes very quiet. Twirling bits of Louise's hair in her fingers.

'You look nice today, Louise.'

'Do you like them?'

Mrs O'Reilly nibbling her little sandwiches. Cocking her head to one side. 'They're sweet.'

After the FreezerWorld robbery Louise was scared of Mr Tens. Her mother knew she was frightened of something and waited patiently for her daughter to say what was on her mind. Stroking her hair. Encouraging her to read books. Always on the lookout for a book her daughter would read all the way through. Taking her to the pictures. Never probing, but making it clear she knew something was up. Eventually, Louise just said there had been a robbery from her till and Mr Tens was being funny with her.

The next morning Mrs O'Reilly insisted on coming with her daughter to FreezerWorld. Grabbed Louise's arm and walked straight into Mr Tens's office without knocking. He was sitting on his managerial chair, bent over a calculator and a pile of stock sheets. A Bible open next to him with two paragraphs highlighted in yellow ink.

'Hello, Mrs O'Reilly.' Mr Tens likes Louise's mother. He points to a chair for her to sit down, but she doesn't want to. Tells him how her daughter is feeling a bit put out about the robbery being from her till. The Express Robbery. It's not her fault, after all, is it? She went for her tea break like every other member of staff. 'Louise wants to be good at her job, Mr Tens. So I've come to clear the air.'

Mr Tens has stopped smiling now. Yes, he muses, it was unfortunate. The thing is, Louise doesn't stand much chance of being promoted to the trolley tills in the short term. He's put her back on the floor. But that is a very responsible job. The floor staff who stock the shelves and freezers keep FreezerWorld running smoothly. That's the whole point. Mr Tens is talking like he's just learnt his script off by heart.

Mrs O'Reilly helps him out. 'FreezerWorld is a plentiful world. Everyone can have a piece of it.'

Mr Tens looks pleased with that line. 'Thank you, Mrs O'Reilly, I'll make a note of that. Remember, though—' Mr Tens smiling at Louise now – 'it's the floor staff who have to fill in the holes and gaps so customers never feel there is something missing from FreezerWorld. Louise has a very important role to play here. The customer must never be encouraged to feel insecure. They know they can put their worries to one side when they're in the store because they know everything they need is there for them.' Mr Tens pauses, it's like he's forgotten what to say next.

Mrs O'Reilly prompts him. 'What they can't have one week because of budget considerations, they know next week it will still be there waiting for them and they deserve to have it.'

Mr Tens agrees. Exactly. He, Mr Tens, is just the architect of FreezerWorld. It's the floor staff that have to wear the hard hats. Mr Tens is sort of like God. He has to make and remake FreezerWorld every week. In the beginning was the word and the word has to sell the product. There will not only be light, there will be light designed to sell canned fish. Mr Tens has to know which way the customer will look, which way the customer will walk, he has to create the shopping body: smelling, tasting, touching, fantasising about possessing items that are a little bit out of their reach. Mr Tens has to make sure that FreezerWorld is a happy world to visit because the customer buys more when she's happy. 'So never underestimate the floor staff, Mrs O'Reilly. This is a short-term blip in Louise's promotion. As long as she works hard and diligently, there is a good future for her at FreezerWorld.'

Mr Tens looks at his watch. 'Seven fifty-five, Louise. I think you should go down now and change into your overalls. We've got a delivery of Argentinian Syrah – that's wine, Mrs O'Reilly – arriving any minute.'

Louise kisses her mother goodbye for the day. They still always kiss when they're going to be away from each other. Every time Louise brings home a FreezerWorld chicken bought with her staff discount card, she feels really good to be looking after her mother. Her mother is everything. She owes her shiny hair to Mrs O'Reilly's gentle hands.

Louise hovers outside the door to make sure Mr Tens is not going to shout at her mother. No one, *no one* is going to treat her mother bad. She'll kill them. That's all. Dead them. If it wasn't for Mrs O'Reilly, she'd still be sick and shivering in a sleeping bag on the streets.

It's all right in there. Mr Tens definitely likes her. Saying something how she's a bit slow with the unpacking, but he's keeping an eye on her. 'I make sure Louise takes her breaks and knows what to do when she gets back. Not to worry, Mrs O'Reilly.'

Nothing to worry about.

The pink hair slides. Mrs O'Reilly fiddled about with the little hearts in Louise's hair. Rearranged them. And then she saw the orange ankle boots. Did Danny buy them? No.

So her girl's getting her own style worked out, is she? A bit of get-up-and-go? That's good. Her girl needs a bit of gingering up; they're cheerful, aren't they? Time to have something to eat. Mrs O'Reilly wants her daughter to have an early night.

Louise is lying to her mother for the first time ever. And more lies coming up. It can't be helped, it really can't. The Louise tangle. Mr England is going to have to fork out, FreezerWorld bank notes on the table *and* answer her questions. Cos she likes the brother and sister. She wants to spend time with them. Like the girl said. Have a laugh. But they fucked it. They'd better watch out. Giving her things and trashing Danny. Louise never forgets. Never. Her head is not full of holes like some people. Mrs O'Reilly is stroking Louise's arm. The one with Mr England's address on it. Calming her girl. Asking her again if there's something on her mind?

9

Merc Madness. Raj has gone berserk. He can't leave the Merc alone. He's bribing his brother to look after the shop for him. Raj's brother is only nine. Can hardly add up. Raj's family are losing out. The more Merc meddling he does, the more he finds to do. He's obsessed. Doesn't care that his brother sold a glass jar of bolognese sauce and two boxes of teabags for twelve pence. Word has got out. Stupid Club has increased its membership. Especially when Raj's brother is on the till. The new Stupid Club topic is about leaves. How in late autumn, beginning of winter, the leaves from the hedges fall onto the pavement. The refuse collectors aren't going to take them away, are they? And the man that sweeps the street on Mondays doesn't sweep the leaves, he just sweeps the litter. He doesn't see leaves as being litter. That means Stupid Club have to walk over the leaves on their way back from the corner shop. Well, if you're not looking where you're going, you can trip over the leaves. If you're walking your dog to the corner shop, he gets the leaves stuck in his paws, doesn't he? Before you know it, the house is full of leaves. Indoors has become just like outdoors. What's the point of having a house if it looks like outdoors? It just takes a bit of rain to exacerbate the situation. Wet leaves are an accident waiting to happen. Easy to slip, break a leg or sprain your ankle, the next thing you know you're in the hospital using up a bed that someone who needs a bone-marrow transplant could have had if it wasn't for the local leaf situation.

No wonder Raj's baby brother wants to get rid of Stupid Club any way he can. He'd give away the entire contents of his dad's shop just to get them out. They should stop taking their pills and eat more sugar and pork fat. Thing is, they've got relatives. The Stupid gene lives on. Raj has given his brother some advice about Stupid Club. What to do when he feels he's losing a grip on his good upbringing. First thing is to turn all the heating in the shop up full. Try to boil 'em out. But that didn't work because Stupid Club rallied to the challenge. Put on T-shirts and shorts every time they ventured out to the corner shop. Stood around wiping the sweat off their cheeks, sharing a bottle of water, in this together, enjoying themselves while Raj and his brother suffered the rage of their father when he got his gas bill. So Raj bought his brother a pile of comics and some earplugs. He knows what exposure to Stupid Club is like. He's got two more suggestions to make and then he must get on with cleaning out the carburettor. One: If their lips move in your direction, just say 'That's only right, isn't it?' Say it every time. Get them used to the routine. Don't ever say anything else. Two: He'll ask their father to contact Amnesty.

Sometimes Billy makes him special pizzas and takes them out, sizzling hot in the baking tin. Raj has been very complimentary about his pizzas, which is good for Billy's pizza confidence. Raj has worked out that every pizza is worth two pounds fifty. When he delivers his Merc bill to Billy, eventually, he'll knock off all the pizzas he's eaten – only fair and square. Could Billy just stick to cheese and tomato?

Billy's got other plans. What about the work he's done on Raj? As far as he's concerned, Raj needs a few parts mending and all.

If Falstaff, a Shakespeare bloke, boasted that he could 'turn diseases to commodity', Billy doesn't see why he shouldn't use his special gifts to buy him a few things he needs. Pain is his triumph. He's going to take Raj through the ethics of pain management, teach him how to tightrope-walk above the abyss. Thing is, Raj doesn't think there *is* an abyss to tiptoe over. Okay, so Stupid Club is the peril of a small business in the English community, but it's not like he's raving. Why then, Billy insists, does Raj think a bloody finger, caught on a bit of metal under the Merc, is a sign of good luck? Is it pain rapture or what? Like the saints who actively seek out pain humiliations of the flesh? No, as far as Billy is concerned, Raj's bloody finger is a dialogue with the spiritual, a damning of the material world with its vain pleasures. Isn't that right, Raj? Eh?

Raj just says something about pasting *Baywatch* stickers onto the Merc when it's ready.

Truth is, at the moment, Raj would rather chat to Girl. In fact, his father bursts into heaving fits of hilarity every time her name comes up. He recalls the time Girl asked him whether Mars Bars came from Mars.

'She was just having you on, Dad,' Raj insists.

'No.' His father shakes his head, spluttering into his handkerchief. 'I'm going to give you some advice, son, lay off the pizzas, they're giving you a paunch. Eat your mother's food. Give the car wreck back to them. If you work in the shop every Sunday for a year, I'll *buy* you a car *with* an engine. As for the girl, she's stark raving bonkers.' There's no insanity in the family and he wants to keep it that way.

The English are famous for being mad. Even the beef is mentally unbalanced, hopping about the asylums (listed buildings) singing hey nonnie no. Less frivolously, and at this point his father takes his wife's hand and squeezes it tight, if he gets wind that his eldest son is getting serious with Crazy Daisy, they'll *find* him a wife.

'But *I'm* English, Dad, and I'm all right.' Raj looks a bit nervous now. Worst of all, he's getting pizza cravings. Wakes up in the middle of the night longing for a Billy Special.

When Girl comes out to 'help' Raj, which means lying stretched out on her back on the bonnet while he fiddles with the clutch, his heart beats a bit faster.

He's forgiven her the chicken-tikka joke. Every Friday something of a tradition has commenced. Girl brings him out a new cocktail, the most recent, presented to him in 'an old-fashioned glass'. She was extra proud of this one. An Apricot Lady, three parts rum, two parts apricot brandy etc., garnished with an orange slice. It sent his head spinning under the car, his fingers went feeble and he cut his thumb, didn't he? Hence the blood that Billy found so interesting. Raj saw it as a good-luck omen regarding his future with Girl. Couldn't say *that* to the lust object's brother, could he? Had to listen to the 'dialogue with the spiritual' analysis and pretend to take notes.

Girl's gone apricot mad. Not just Fridays, every week day there's an apricot theme. Apricot fizz, apricot shake, apricot sour, apricot sparkler. Raj has had to familiarise himself with different kinds of cocktail glasses just to please Girl. A chilled highball glass. A chilled collins glass. A chilled fucking this, a chilled fucking that. It's a relief to grab a Pepsi from his dad's shop fridge and glug it extra quick to halt the cocktail thirst rasping his throat, whirling his brain, whacking his thumbs into Merc tin. Raj doesn't dare put a price on the cocktails. They are either free or priceless. A grey area. Raj is confused. Got to get his younger brother to take a swig after a hard day of Stupid Club tolerance and get his point of view.

Mind you, Billy and Girl really appreciate his work. Billy

calls Raj the Michelangelo of Merc. It's an art treasure, the pizza boy swoons. 'I've lost my equilibrium, I'm scared of falling, it's a sightseeing rapture, I want to write postcards to people I don't know describing it. A beauty catastrophe, better than Venice, my Merc pain inheritance.'

Girl is much cooler. 'Yeah, Raj, it's getting there.' Where is there? Raj wants to know. Girl brought another blonde to look at it. Give her opinion. Louise.

Louise is wonderful. Two blondes in a day. She wears these far-out orange ankle boots. Louise reckons the Merc is nearly there too. Gave him a blow job on the back seat. Aaaah. This is the life. Don't ever tell Girl. It's a secret for ever. He wasn't asking for it. She just did it. Touching him in the dark with the smell of petrol between them. Made a feast of him. Not just peckish, Louise was starving. Aaah. Life is good. Next morning he wiped the seat with apricot creme cleaning fluid, to keep up with the apricot theme Girl had introduced into his lifestyle. It's Girl he wants, but she's not offering and he's not pushing. Her lips. 'Kiss me soon but not now' lips. There to be kissed but she doesn't know how to ask and he's not agitating. Anyway he has to keep his Girl feelings secret from his family. Especially since they all seem to have become involved in the car, and make lame excuses to visit him while he's working on it. Which is most of the time. Merc Madness.

His uncle has offered to re-upholster the seats with the purple velveteen reject sample from his factory. Not to be outdone, his auntie has given him a number of air fresheners in the shape of apples and pears and Christmas trees to hang from the mirror. What with the *Baywatch* stickers and the tastes and opinions of three owners, plus Raj's family putting their oar in on a regular basis, it's going to be one hell of a crowded car. If Raj can pull it off, he's going to build a minibar in the back for Girl.

Someone else has come to see the car and Raj doesn't know how he feels about it. His first identifiable feeling was fear. Louise's mother came to see the car and Raj's voice came out a bit too high when she introduced herself. She appeared the day after Louise gave him the first blow job he'd ever had. Mrs O'Reilly. Rajindra. When he uttered his name he visibly shook. Sex repercussions about to happen. He hadn't even asked for it, Louise had made the suggestion and he thought it was quite a good one. Perhaps he should scarper into the shop on the pretext of taking over from his little brother on the till? But Mrs O'Reilly made him stay with her gentle womanly manner. Introduced herself with a little smile and looked interested when he showed her round the Merc and all his improvements. Yes, she thought purple velveteen would 'give a lovely feeling' to the car, thanked him politely for taking time out to show her his craftsmanship, thank you very much and she has to rush because she's off to fetch her daughter from work. She and Louise are going to the pictures. Yes, she wouldn't mind a couple of pies from Raj's father's shop because her girl might be peckish after a hard day at work. Louise has an insatiable appetite. Raj muttering something about the weather, a bit rainy if she knows what he means, ushering her into the shop, instructing her to push through Stupid Club towards the fridge, waving goodbye.

After she left, Raj felt a sudden stabbing pain in his abdomen. It just came over him from nowhere. Mrs O'Reilly saying goodbye. It was a difficult and perplexing moment, the burden of some kind of affliction weighing her down, shining through her cheerfulness, something so sad that even Stupid Club went silent for a few seconds. That was a real first. The thing Stupid Club hates most is silence. Whenever silence seems inevitable, Stupid Club have been known to move as one unit towards a packet of Hula Hoops and read out loud all the ingredients listed on the back, provoking an intense discussion on the virtues of starch salt.

Raj suddenly wants to have access to a multiplicity of understandings. He feels that his youth has been exposed to personal anguish and transgression and that in some odd way he has grown up. He even feels sad on behalf of Stupid Club. That night he went to bed early, took a couple of aspirins and dreamt of black rain gushing from his eyes. In the morning he'd forgotten all about it, ate his cornflakes and left the house whistling.

10

Louise made sure she scrubbed Mr England's address off her arm before she visited him. She copied it onto a scrap of paper which she immediately lost. Big panic. Sleepless nights. Packing the FreezerWorld fridges like a robot with fear fever programmed into its inners. What if her mother finds it? Well, so what if her mother finds it? Louise has a special understanding with her mother. Never to lie to her. Louise has broken faith and she feels bad inside. The bad feeling is like a thin silver needle in her flesh, it hurts every time she moves. Yesterday she couldn't go into work and her mother had to phone Mr Tens.

'Is there something worrying you, Louise?'

Louise shaking her head, letting her mother, who is perched on the side of her bed, brush out the tangles in her hair, stroking her cheeks, fussing over her. It is very important to her mother that Louise is all right. The agreement is that if Louise is not all right, she'll tell her mother, who will do everything she can to make her all right. More than all right. Everything that her mother can control in the world, to do with Louise, she will. Every detour from what she knows, every journey to the turbulent geography of her daughter's inner life she has to make, every astonishing nightmare she has to understand as if it is her own, this is her project for whatever is left of her motherly life.

She wants the pain in Louise to settle. Her image for it is like the fake snow in those paperweights with Christmas scenes inside them. It is very important that Louise is not shaken. Louise's body contains multiple pain pathways. It is entirely necessary for her face to appear to be impassive and emotionless. Start feeling a little at a time. That's what her mother says to her. Eat the elephant in bite-sized mouthfuls.

Louise and her mother chewing the elephant, gargling with Tizer afterwards.

Mr England. Louise was clever, she found him with only the dimmest memory of his address. Danny drove her all the way there. Took the day off work and crawled up and down one particular street in Nottingham. Louise pointed to the door she thought was more than likely the entrance to Mr England's castle. Despite the fear fever that had set in, she always knew she would find him. Told Danny to wait in the car, she would be about forty minutes at the most.

Danny wasn't worried cos he had the local newspaper with him. Danny is crazy for the Lonely Hearts section of any publication. Likes to read how people describe what they want. 'Sartre seeks De Beauvoir: a mentally elegant and clear-eyed mature woman for gentle cultural activities.' Yeah? Not exactly. Not for him. He's not a Lonely Heart anyway, it's just recreation. He's got Louise and she takes up all his time. Completely out of it. But he loves her. Most of the time. He told her mother so. 'I love your girl, Mrs O'Reilly. What a fucking dream queen but she's got to me.' All of them looking after her. Mr Tens the Christian. Got God in a big way, has Mr Tens. Plays golf with the Christian Sportsman Club. All of them looking out for Louise. After Mrs O'Reilly explained to them how she found her adopted daughter. Runaway teenage grief mess. Snot and tears and a little pink lipstick hidden in her Chinese silk purse. Mrs O'Reilly loves Louise and so does

Danny the dog prince. He loves fucking her and she loves fucking him.

There she is, knocking on the door dressed in her orange ankle boots and matching orange mohair miniskirt her new friend has given her. Louise is changing on a daily basis. Wears her hair up now, little heart and butterfly clips all over her blondness, even painted her fingernails orange – which Mr Tens gave her a lecture about. Mr Tens the Christian. Danny knows him because they were at school together. Titchy Tens was in the sixth form when he was just a second-year learning how to smoke in the toilets. Even then Terry Tens had started the Christian club. 'Oh, come o-n, Ter-ry, oh, co-me o-n, Te-r-ry, if you're a ten take down your drawers and prove it, oh, come and adore it, oh, come and adore it.'

Yeah, she's gone in now. Some bloke in a lumberjack shirt opened the door.

Mr England. Handsome. A big man in a checked shirt. The kind of shirt healthy men wear in the cigarette ads. He still had his hair. Styled like a rocker, greased back with long sideburns. Said he was trying out a new product called Bière d'Alsace. A full-flavoured premium-quality lager. A charmer who had to lean against walls on account of his enthusiasm for the new product. Banging into the corridor walls, smearing his hair grease over the cheery sunflower wallpaper.

What did she want? Louise felt the right side of all right because she had nothing to lose. Except the love of her mother and she had already risked that when she broke faith. Nothing left apart from that. Nothing makes you reckless. She just fucking barged in. He followed her. Walking straight into the lounge room with its TV blaring and empty bottles strewn on the immaculately hoovered carpet. Apart from the bottles the place was spotless. A tatty Elvis poster above the mantelpiece. Elvis when he was old and fat, groaning into the mike. Mr England pointing his beer bottle at the TV screen. Said he liked watching the American chat shows. Could always tell which audience member was going to do something outrageous like take their clothes off for the studio cameras.

Yep, he's been watching a lot of TV recently. Funny how the most popular presenters put the audience down – he especially enjoys it when they put the guest celebrities 'in a tight corner.' Celebrities are just tanned targets in nice clothes, aren't they?

So how does Mr England identify the lone crazy in the studio then? Oh, just a little talent of his. Louise with her blue eyes. Blue for danger. 'So what do you think I am going to do next then, Mr England?'

He opens another bottle of his d'Alsace beer and takes in her orange mohair body. The cute little clips in her hair. 'I used to meet girls like you when I drove lorries.' He's trying to keep himself together, distracted but half enjoying himself, not got the strength to chuck her out. 'Oh, yeah? And what were the girls like?' 'Oh, (making his voice amused) they used to admire the big teddy bear he hung on the roof of his vehicle, it was his good-luck motif, every trucker had something for luck. Some of the girls used to take the teddy bear down and cuddle it. They just wanted something to cuddle, didn't they?'

'Oh, yeah?' Well, she doesn't like teddy bears, does she? Their glass eyes freak her out. Their nylon fur makes her sneeze. The little stitched-on paws make her cry for no good reason. So how else is she like the girls he gave lifts to?

The big man hides his face in his beer. Forget it. Was a long time ago. It's history now. Would she like some cheese on toast?

Yeah, she would. That would do her fine, as it happens.

Been a long journey. No, she won't wait in the front room, she'll talk to him in the kitchen while he makes her that little snack. By the way, her name is Louise.

That information stopped him in his tracks. Zigzag tracks of electrified wire volting through him. Sizzling him. Singeing his eyebrows. 'Did you say Louise?'

'Yeah.'

'Louise.' He straightens up a bit. Tries to say something but he can't. Just staring into the d'Alsace label on the bottle. Stands completely still and silent. His eyes full of terror and beer tears. 'I've not got any bread.'

'Well, don't fucking offer me cheese on toast then.'

Mr England walks back to the front room, banging his head on the door. 'Sometimes I cook up a feast. Know what that is, Louise?'

Louise shakes her head. Glad the TV is on. Something to look at so she doesn't have to stare at him all the time.

'I fry myself a bit of road rat.' He points at a gormless bloke on the TV. 'Him, you see him, the one in the Pizza Hut T-shirt? He's going to take off his kit any minute. I bet you a tenner he's going to streak right in front of the cameras.'

The magnified image of the TV man. Blowing his nose into a king-sized handkerchief. Not a looker like Mr England with his hairstyle and well-pressed shirt. 'Sometimes I cook myself a cheeseburger just like Elvis's cook used to make him. See, Louise, every Elvis song is about loss.' The Pizza Hut bloke jumps up and his trousers fall round his ankles.

Louise stands right in front of the television. Time for the facts.

'I've come for my share of the money.'

'What money?'

'The money Billy and Girl gave you.'

Mr England looks amazed. 'What's it to do with you?'

'They got it from my till, see. Express.'

'Is that right?'

'Yeah. It is fucking right, Mr England. So give me two hundred quid and I'll go.'

He's sobering up now. 'I don't know anything about your till or whatever. I sold them a car. You got to get the money off them.'

'Naaaaa. You took it all, didn't you? Took the whole fucking lot off your kids.'

DONT FUCK ABOUT. PUT THE NOTES ON THE TABLE.

Mr England is staring at her moist-eyed now. 'I ain't got nothin' for ya,' he croons in a good ol' Southern boy voice, unbuttoning his healthy man shirt. Revealing a spotless white vest. 'I haven't got any of the money. It's gone. I had a few debts, Louise.'

Throwing the shirt on the carpet over the bottles. Taking off his vest. Turned away from her so she can only see the slack muscles turned to fat. A broad back. Turning towards her now. Full of self-exhaustion, the world-weariness of an ex-heart-throb.

Dad is just a hole. He hasn't got a chest. Putting his face close to hers. She can see the scars on his face now. His face has been built up. Layers of skin taken from his chest and put on his face. Layers of skin scraped from his chest.

'See, Louise. My girl set fire to me.'

'I did, didn't I?' Louise replies.

'I lost my own flesh. I don't owe nothing.'

'I did, didn't I?' Louise says again.

'Ey?' Mr England completely bewildered. He's backing away. Moving his hands over the holes in his chest. A man full of holes. A manhole.

'You're not Louise,' he whispers.

'I am.'

'You're not *my* Louise.'

Louise is shaken. Snow falling over the Christmas scene. She's on a pain pathway. Can't get off it.

'I'm as evil as a blonde can get,' she whispers.

'What you saying?'

'I said I'm as evil as a blonde can get.'

The mister, the man, ghost Dad, manhole, something man staring at her, all beer and confusion, the smouldering bits of him, burning up, combusting.

'Go on. Say it to me.'

'Say what?'

'Say you're as evil as a blonde can get.'

Mr England searching for his vest. Staggering about for his checked lumberjack shirt. Louise has placed her orange boot over it and he doesn't dare ask her to move. He's been here before. Girl Danger announcing itself. The holeman remembers.

'You're as evil as a blonde can get.'

'Say it more.'

'You're as evil as a blonde can get.'

'Say it over and over.'

'You're as evil as a blonde can get evil as a blonde can get evil as a blonde evil evil can get.'

He stops. Some kind of knowledge pulling through the manhole. 'I'm not your dad, Louise. You know I'm not. Pull yourself together now. C'mon now, there's a good girl.'

'I can't.'

'You can. It's happening. I can see it's beginning. I'm *not* him, okay? I don't think you're evil.'

Louise sobbing into her see-thru cleavage. 'Where's their Mom?'

'I don't know. I don't know.'

'You got to tell me for *them*.'

He grabs his shirt and starts to struggle into it, taking his time, doing up the buttons at his own pace. Wiping the beer off his lips with the back of his hand. Forget the gas fire and brown hundred per cent wool carpet. It doesn't stand for anything. It's what's inside that matters. He is a rugged individualist, with a past. The stranger who swings open the saloon doors and the guys at the bar know he's seen a bit. Been through it. Don't ask any questions. A loner, living in the suburbs with coyotes and his horse. Except this is the moment Mr England has been dreaming about these past few years. He's played it over and over in his head. Practised his TV interview to the nation till he knows exactly what he's going to say. If he imagines the cameras are rolling he can get across his point of view. Mr England makes an attempt to get a media-friendly tone into his voice. Preparing himself to touch the hearts of the five-o'clock viewing population. Puts a comb through his hair. Rubs his hands over his face. Does a few excercises to relax his jaw. Makes sure he's sitting straight and not like some slob from Bumford. Checks out where the cameras would be if they were actually there. Positions them in his head so he never looks straight at them. Takes a deep breath. Caressing Louise with his eyes, and, by implication, the viewing public. Best to use everything you got in this life.

'I don't know why I'm supposed to be the big bad wolf in all of this. Up to a point I'll take my share. I'll take fifty per cent but not a hundred. Like Elvis said, I wasn't made to be married. I don't like it. Husband walking around farting. Wife walking around scratching. Kids going around hollering. Yes, I hit my lad because he ran away with my wife. In a manner of speaking, you understand. I'm not a basket case. I was out of order. But he provoked me.' Dad pauses. Shaking his handsome head at the pathos and beauty of being a dysfunctional. 'I loved my wife. She used to have a beehive and that. After the birth of the lad, I lost her. She had eyes only for him. I went on an eating binge. Stuffing myself with mashed potato and gravy, nine Suffolk porkers in one sitting followed by a packet of biscuits.'

Louise doesn't know how to conduct this interview. What tone of voice or questions to ask. She doesn't even know about bringing in the studio McPsychologist to tell the nation how Mr England did not have a reliable role model for fatherhood and masculinity. Boring. Well, if it's so damn fucking boring, why are they all watching?

Information to make the viewers gawp, coming up.

'My girl, my daughter, twelve years old, I loved her above myself, would have done anything for her, my little princess, even though she was a secret smoker, set fire to me after I went a bit far with the lad. I went to have a lie-down. My girl poured paraffin over my head, set fire to me with my very own Elvis lighter, the one with "Don't Be Cruel" printed on it. A collector's item. *No one* helped me. Not the lad, not the wife, not the daughter, not the neighbours. The bed sheets on fire. By the time the ambulance finally pulled up with a puncture and three so called medics – poets in white coats who'd just done a first-aid course – I was nearly gone. They carried me on a stretcher down the stairs trying to work out what rhymes with dead.'

The nation holds its breath. That's quite something, isn't it?

Mr England thinks he's doing well. When the time comes for the real cameras he'll be well rehearsed. Word-perfect.

'My wife took the blame, didn't she? Said she was provoked. Got a doctor's report on the boy's bruises. They let her off, but she wasn't allowed to stay with her kids. Had to live separate. Her father's looking after them.'

141

Mr England looks directly into the lightbulb so tears will roll down his cheeks.

'Yes, I have had a few girlfriends since. Thing is, I never like to go to sleep with them in the house. It's a panic thing. Case they do something to me while I'm sleeping.' Mr England shifts his focus. Imagines where the McPsychologist will be sitting. Should he give him a sly wink? Probably a few housewives out there who want to marry him. Credits coming up. Chat-show theme tune coming up.

'Look, fuck off, will you? I haven't a clue where their mother is. Piss off out of my house now. Any more trouble from my family sending people over here, I'll hire a security guard. Going to put a sign on my door: ARMED RESPONSE.'

'Yeah?'

Louise believes him. He hasn't a clue. Got no curiosity. Mr England has shut himself in his castle for ever. Patiently tying the bin liners with little strips of green plastic wire. Doing his weekly shop for one. Pint of milk and little tin of butter beans. Watching the chat shows. Singing old Elvis numbers. She's got no information for the girl and Billy. Billy's voice coming into her head. Telling her about the man who gave a name to his pain. Called it dog. Kicked and screamed at it. She can't find a name for her pain. 'They' hurt her and she ran away. Princess Louise of FreezerWorld. Cooling down – calmed by the murmuring. Fridges humming Louise lullabies to her broken heart, all day long. Hush little baby don't say a word. Hush little baby. Hush. Atgam, Cleocin, Didrex, Povera Quinidine, glass vials, white gloves, Lidocaine, Darvocet, Phenurone, diagnostic manuals, the free market, free love or the essential English dictionary, they're not going to do it. Mrs O'Reilly might just do it. Taking her in. Folding her into her Mom arms. Cleaning up the snot and tears. Yeah, the Girl and Billy voice channelling through her as one voice, they're in this together. What did Girl say? 'Soon all the kids in England will be pushing up daisies.'

Someone's knocking at the door. Ringing the bell.

Mr England looks worried now. Punching his fist into his own thigh.

'Only Danny.' Louise lets him in, princess eyes squeezed into pain slits. Biting her nails.

'You all right, Lou?' Danny, who's taken the day off work on her behalf and everything.

'I'm all right.'

Mr England just about manages to stand up and stagger to the corridor. Complete fucking strangers coming to his house. It's got to stop. Why's the bloke staring at him like that? Mr England slugging another premium lager.

Danny checking him out. Sneaking side glances at Louise. He's used to getting into situations with her. She's a wild girl. Knows he mustn't ask too many questions. Sometimes you can't, got to keep ventilation between knowing and not knowing when you love someone. Ask when you have to, otherwise leave it. Danny's never believed he has to know everything. I mean, he's not some fucking private dick on the Louise File, is he? Louise. Danny loves the smell of her hair. Holding her tight in her bad times. A man in love. Walking proud, heart busting with Louise. Teenage runaway. Those orange ankle boots the other girl gave her. He was just pretending when he said he liked them but it all went wrong because she believed him and he didn't want to be cruel. There are limits to love. It's not good for a bloke to have a girlfriend who looks like Marc Bolan.

Billy

The Merc is now 'all there'. It's a good thing I've got my books and pain research to keep me preoccupied because I've stopped talking. My voice is in hiding and only Mom is going to drag it kicking and screaming out of me. This happened ever since Raj kissed my crazy bitch sister in the back seat of the Merc. Look, Raj is not just my best friend, he is also a patient. I've been working on him for some time which is why I didn't pay a penny when he delivered his bill for the motor. I couldn't anyway because Grand-Dad cash has stopped. We have not received an envelope for two weeks now. The two-thirty has not come home. It's probably being mashed up for cat food because in all this time Grand-Dad has never not sent us cash.

Look, if my sister gets intimate with Raj, it's like me getting intimate with him, and that's not ethical. Never ever sleep with your patients. Go down that road and you're a professional without a profession, an omelette without eggs. Time to take myself off to a film. Sit in the dark. Take out my lickle Billy knife and slide it into the seat. It's known as 'cutting' in the mind trade. I have been looking into this knife thing, come to a few conclusions if you've got the time to hear me out? I think my little knife is to protect me from being castrated by my mother. Yep, I'll wait while you fix yourself a Pernod and open the cocktail-hour Twiglets. See, if anyone's gonna castrate this boy, it's gonna be me. Gonks. If ever there was a castrated pet toy it's the gonk. Grew its hair long to cover the severed parts. Honky Gonky. A mummie's gonk.

I have become my mother in order to prevent my own castration. Someone get me some gripe water, quick! Mom has disappeared but she blinks in my mind all through the night. She never goes to sleep. I study myself through the watchful eyes of my absent mother. She fills the whole screen with her big eye sockets, watching me. Where I score, tho', is I don't feel like I'm the wicked son waiting to be punished, nor do I want to destroy her power. I just want some of it. *No one* is cutting off my dick. *No one* is even going to lop off my foreskin for religious purposes. One thing I'm sure of: my dick is bigger than Dad's was. Heh heh heh. Let me explain myself. What I am saying to the distinguished gentlemen assembled here (the local Odeon, as it happens) is that I have access to more masculinities than Dad. I am husband, father, son, brother, virgin, pimp, career man, *homme fatale* – yep, I'll wait while you pour yourself another vodka martini. Got any frankfurters? I am a wizard, a vampire, a smart boy with pain problems. So when I cut up the seats, it's Mom trying to castrate me.

Velvet cinema seats made for watching heroes and heroines fall in and out of love. Girl and I are made for the big screen. We are hero and heroine material and there will probably be a car chase on account of us now having a car because Raj is expressing himself motor manually.

The reason why we are heroic is because we are tragic and flawed. Yep. If there is some kind of catharsis to be had in the future I hope it's got antiseptic and yards of sterilised gauze waiting for us at the end of it. I have this idea that perhaps the Merc will be like James Dean's Porsche Spyder. We'll have an accident, a smash-up, and die young. Word of the tragedy will echo around the world. We will be icons of the alcoholic-lemonade generation. Someone will unearth photographs of us and become famous. A number of these early pics will wind up in the Museum of Modern Art in New York and in the table-tennis club in Rotherham. I want the Merc to smash on account of Girl and Raj. Lost my sister and my patient/best friend in one sitting. I'm not going to ever speak again.

When Raj beeped the born-again Merc hooter, Girl and I were wringing our hands in the kitchen because Grand-Dad has let us down. No money to even do a shop and we are big consumers. We need to shop. Shopping for us is like going on a long walk in the countryside. We feel healthier afterwards. We sleep better. Breathe easy. Even if food rots in our fridge, at least we know it is there. Even if cleaning products are never used and gather dust in the cupboard under the sink, we feel all the more clean for owning them. So we are moody when we go outside to see what all the fuss is about. Frankly, we don't give a fuck about anything at the moment. Grand-Dad, despite his humour problems, equals survival. The world is about to lose Billy England to malnutrition. While the mediocre stuff themselves with mushroom pies and straight men with a famine of masculinities at their fingertips write literary novels in their second homes in France and their wives bring up the kiddies, Billy England is about to die.

Raj beeping the horn again.

There he is! Raj put our pain inheritance into intensive care and today the master surgeon is wearing a new silk shirt to celebrate new Merc life. Revving the engine, his elbow out of the window and a fat Cuban cigar between his fingers.

'C'mon in,' he drawls in this new self-satisfied voice. My crazy fucked sister. A moment ago she was talking about us drowning ourselves in a canal somewhere, and now she's opening the Merc door like she's taking a spin to her health club. She sits next to Raj (purple velveteen seats) who shows her the work he's done 'on all the controls' (like this is an aeroplane or something) and then, worst of all, takes her into the back seat where he's built her a minibar. A minibar! Raj, who is not only wearing a silk shirt but also new Nikes in the shape of spats, puts his arm around my sister while she fiddles about with the hundreds of miniatures some cousin has given him.

'Hey, Billy man, drive us somewhere.'

Whaat? He knows I can't drive. For a start there are so many beads and air fresheners in the shape of apples, weird Gods and pears hanging from the mirror, I can't see out of the front window. Raj coming on like some French playboy from one of those crummy old movies set in a casino, watching Girl mix the miniatures, shake the mixer and pour 'em both some killer brew, forgetting all about *me*! Raj knocking it back in one *and* then kissing my bitch sister full on the lips for about two three four minutes.

What am I supposed to do? Watch? Drive off? Make notes? Go away discreetly on the big day of our Merc delivery? Four minutes is a long time if you live your life intensely. Four minutes. Enough time to let silence fall eloquently over the proceedings. I mean, the Merc is supposed to be one third mine. Seems like the back seat ain't big enough for three.

12

Louise feels really hard done by. So she calls on the England children and tells them the truth. Their dad doesn't know anything. Got no information for them. They're gawping at her, not believing her, making her feel bad. Worst of all, Billy has stopped talking. Passes little notes across the table to her. HOW MANY TIMES DID YOU ASK DAD WHERE MOM WAS? COME ON! ONE TWO THREE TIMES? WHAT? She can't even read his writing. Girl has to lean over, swipe the note and read it out loud, making her feel stupid. Who the fuck do they think they are? Girl wants to know what they talked about. Did she get the right house? How can she be sure? Did Dad give her a message for his kiddies? No? Is Louise keeping something back from them? If she is, she better spill the beans. Billy shaking his head. Insinuating she handled it really badly. That she's no good. Girl snarling at her. The Louise tangle. Okay, what did Dad do when Louise said her name was Louise? But Louise isn't good at describing things. She doesn't like setting the scene. It's not her thing.

'He said you set fire to him,' Louise says in a morbid, expressionless voice. 'For bashing Billy.'

Girl puts her hand on her lip. 'I did, didn't I?'

Her brother nods. Writes something. FANKS. THANKS.

Girl's face starts to cave in on her. The whole Girl thing collapsing. 'Oh, my God!'

Billy writing more. NO GOD. JUST PAIN.

Tears. Girl's tears are hideous. Pouring out of her. She's

sobbing into her hands, meowling, even her hair is wet, red welts on her cheeks where she rubs them and cries more.

'I'm evil, Billy.'

NO EVIL. JUST PAIN.

Girl stamps out of the room. Slamming the door, making everything shake and judder off the shelves, about to fall and break. Everything is trembling at the moment. Juddering to the edge about to fall.

GIRL'S GONE TO SEE RAJ. THEY KISS ALL THE TIME.

Another Billy note. Who do the England kids think they are? Louise has got a hunch that Billy has become even more frightened of his sister. On account of her being capable of damaging someone. Dad. Louise likes it that Billy is afraid. Something she can do too. Damage people. So why not wind him up a bit? She sits at the table making her eyes flutter up to the top of her head. Talks to him with just the whites showing. Makes her voice go croaky so he has to call the exorcist in to number 24. 'I am possessed, Bill-ee, I am possessed, Bill-ee.' Billy's losing it. Taking out his knife. Cutting up the kitchen chairs. Not threatening her. Just doing it to let off steam. He's hungry. Hasn't had a proper meal for weeks. There's no food in the house. Only what Raj gives them from the shop. So Raj has become a bit of a saviour in Girl's eyes, a saviour who does kissing. Billy is losing it. He hasn't made a pizza since Raj kissed Girl. Not seen a movie in weeks. The TV listings bore him sick. No weather to play hoopla in the park, that's what you do, isn't it? Play sports in the open air? Louise is sick of hearing him moan through his notes. Why's he gone dumb? Just because that bloke kissed his sister?

'I'm possessed, Billee! Billeeeeeeeeee! Billeeee.'

Billy just can't believe it. Girl's mad enough, but to have to endure Louise is too much. He opens a book on the psychochemistry of the brain, ignoring the FreezerWorld girl and her retard play-acting.

Two hours after Girl stormed out of number 24 in a whirl of tears, she storms back in with Raj on her arm. Both of them are clutching FreezerWorld bags. Louise finds it hard to believe Girl has dared go back there after robbing Express. But she has. She goes there a lot. Louise sees her skulking in the aisles. Staring at her. She knows Girl follows her home. Watches her when she's out with Danny. She doesn't mind that so much. Girl has taught her a lot. Taken her round the shops, bought her new clothes. Given her new words and thoughts. Louise even helps Girl write her words on walls. Girl doesn't know that Louise does this. MOM CALL HOME. GIRL. Louise has written it quite a few times – whenever she sees a space and no one is looking. Easy.

Raj is a bit shy when he sees Louise on account of their afternoon in the car. Louise has a hunch Girl doesn't know about that. No need to, is there? She enjoyed herself. So she just nods at Raj, who can barely look her in the eye, and she notices that he and Girl suit each other. What with his thick black hair and purple hipsters. Girl with her peroxide blondness and little blue denim minidress. *Denim?* Louise finds herself outraged. *Denim.* How come Girl is wearing denim when she's given so many lectures to Louise about what crap denim is, except in the form of a bikini. A bikini? But there she is, in a denim minidress, her cheeks burning up with Girl fever. What's going on? Fire in her face. Has she gone all the way with Raj? She's saying FreezerWorld thoughts like she always does, always talking about it, obsessed, FreezerWorld is this, FreezerWorld atmosphere, FreezerWorld discount announcements. She takes something out of the FreezerWorld bag and throws it at her brother.

'Eat this snack, Billy boy, I got some news for you.'

Billy grabs the crisps. He's hungry. No Grand-Dad cash. Raj must have lent her some money for a shop. Raj who slaps him on the back in a brotherly way these days. No way to treat your doctor, Raj. There are reasons for formality. Rules to protect you. Learn them.

'All right, man?'

No, Billy is not all right. Choking on the pickled-onion-flavoured potato snax shaped like monster feet.

'Okay. Fasten your straitjackets.' Girl is delirious.

Raj is standing behind her. What for? In case she falls or what? Billy just wants to get a flu virus and go to bed for a week.

'I'm checking out your potato snax, Billy, and this announcement comes over the speakers. Mr Tens making one of his broadcasts. Don't cut out, Billy, listen, come back, you little creep, and don't blank out because what I am saying is . . . BILLY, *Come BACK!* I've found Mom.'

Even Girl's denim dress is steaming. 'Mr Tens goes blah blah blah blah blah and I have a message for Louise: Call your Grand-Dad's local hospital. If his horse hasn't come home it means he's ill. You could be in for some inheritance.'

Billy goes crazy. Stands up and kicks over the bin. Scratches for paper. Labels off old tins. Anything. Starts scribbling, his head too fast for his hand.

'Talk, Billy. We're nearly there. Talk. Fucking talk, we've found her.'

Billy shakes his head sadly. Passes the note to Raj. 'DID YOU HEAR HIM SAY THAT TOO?'

'Sure.' Raj is excited. 'That's what he said.'

'Mr Tens is always saying stuff,' Louise pipes in. 'He goes on like that all day.'

'That was for *us*, Billy. Grand-Dad's in hospital.'

Her brother nods. Kicks the wall. Writes eight words; MOM GAVE HIM THE MESSAGE TO READ OUT.

'Exactly, Billy. Exactly.' Girl turns on Louise. 'Okay, so you fucked up the first time, Louise. You worked on Express and there wasn't enough in the till. And you demanded your share. You fucked up with Dad. Didn't get any information we don't already know. This is your last chance.'

She pushes Raj into a chair, out of the way. Girl wants the whole floor to parade on. Got to clear her mind. No obstacles to trip up on. Except for Louise.

'I did tell you something you didn't know.'

'What?'

'You set fire to your Dad.'

Girl searches for something to say. Like how do you spell flea?

'You did, though, didn't you, Girl?' Raj interrupts.

'I don't know.'

'Billy told me.'

Girl paces round the kitchen. Opening the fridge, shutting it again. Calling the cat even though it ran away months ago.

'We are going to kidnap Mr Tens.'

Billy nodding vigorously. Yeah, of course. No doubt about it. Mr Tens is going to talk. Raj looking unsure. Louise smiling a sick smile.

'We are going to kidnap him this evening and bring him back here.'

Billy writing again. Squeaking and writing: TORTURE HIM TILL HE SAYS WHERE HE GOT GRAND-DAD INFORMATION FROM.

Girl agrees. 'Mr Tens will not take a step out of this house alive unless he tells us who gave him that note. Raj, that person is our mother. Do you understand? She knows something we don't know and she's trying to tell us.'

Raj pokes his finger through one of the pickled-onion-flavoured monster feet. 'Why don't you just ring the hospital and find out what's happened to your grand-dad?'

Girl lights up two menthols. Gives one to Billy. 'Got to preserve our mental stability, Raj.'

'I'll ring him for you.' Raj just can't understand this Grand-Dad hysteria.

Billy writing something again, in between pretending to inhale menthol. 'WOULD PREFER STARVE. EAT CAT ON THIN CRUST.'

The England kids look up at Louise. 'What time does Tens knock off?'

'Nine o' clock.'

Right. Girl turns to Raj. 'Are you up for this, baby?'

'What do you want me to do?'

'Drive us there. Wait while we get him out and put him in the boot. Drive us back here after.'

Raj laughs. Turns to Billy. His old friend. His part-time shrink. Trusting his opinion. Sad to lose the Billy voice over a kiss. Girl told him all about it. How her brother's gone mute since the first kiss. Raj misses him.

'What do you think, Billy?'

Billy takes his time now. Writes very slowly with the pen. When it runs out of ink he licks the nib with his little pink tongue. Starts again. They all wait for him because one day Billy is going to be famous. Got his own pace. His own way through.

RAJ THIS IS THE LAST CHAPTER IN OUR SEARCH FOR MOM. SHE IS VERY CLOSE. WE HAVE TO DO THIS FOR PSYCHIC HELF. HEALTH. OUR STORY IS AN ANCIENT STORY. CHILDREN SEARCHING FOR THEIR FOLK. HELP US. BILLY.

Raj reads, chewing his lip. 'Yip.' He gives Girl the go-ahead look. 'I'll be your driver.'

'Right.' Girl turns on Louise. 'You got to help us too.'

Louise shakes her head. 'Na. Don't want to lose my job.'

Jeeezus. Girl bangs her fists on the table. Everything juddering again. 'Did you hear that? Did you hear her? She doesn't want to lose her job? What job? Being a retard for two pounds seventy-five an hour? Having to listen to Tens talk to her like he found her under a stone somewhere? Doing her a favour? Listen, baby . . .'

Ever since Girl has been consorting amorously with Raj she's taken to calling everyone 'baby'. It's her new love mode and it makes her brother want to grate her cheeks.

'You can do better than FreezerWorld, Louise. Jeezus! You could be a model for a start, couldn't she, Billy?'

Her brother writing something: A MODEL PATIENT.

'He says definitely,' Girl exclaims.

'FreezerWorld is for losers or anthropologists, Louise. Listen, you got the looks. We're working on the posture. Billy's giving your mind a seeing-to. You don't get out of bed for two pounds seventy-five an hour. They pay that to dead people they've dug up and put overalls on.'

Guffaws all round. Except from Louise.

'Listen, Louise.' Girl sits down next to her. For a moment she doesn't look mad. 'We're in this together. You know why, don't you?'

Louise thinks. 'Yeah. We're in this together. But I don't know why.'

'My name is Louise too. Did you know that?'

Louise nods. 'Mr England told me.'

'Right.' Girl tries to rake this whole Louise thing home. Make a nice neat little path right to Louise's mind door.

'There's a Louise inside Girl which is me, right? And there's a girl inside you even tho you're called Louise. Thing is, you are more of a girl than you are Louise. And I am more Louise than

Girl because I'm cleverer than you. It's not that you're stupid, it's that you're stunted, okay? Tho I am Girl I am getting to be more Louise than Girl. Yeah, I know it's difficult, but struggle, Louise. We're doing a Channel swim here, not ten yards, okay? We got to pool our Louiseness. Find something good for both of us. Something that suits. We got to get the most beautiful version of Louise we can find. We got to make her up, baby. I can only become Louise when I find Mom. You need me to find her too. I know you do. We got a bit of work to do before we can count on Louise being a good thing to be.'

'Yeah. I sort of understand.' Louise looks dejected. 'One thing.'

'Whaaaaaaaaaat?' Girl wants to get moving. Kill Mr Tens. Kill Mr Tens.

'Don't slag off Danny.'

'Uh-huh. Yeah, well. What do you see in him?'

'His heart is in the right place.'

'Hmmmmm.' Girl catches Billy's eye. 'Most of us probably got the heart in the right place, Louise. Otherwise we'd be dead or have blue lips all the time.'

'I said *leave him alone*.'

Billy writing again. WHAT DOOR DOES TENS COME OUT OF AT NINE O' CLOCK?

Girl reads the question out for Louise.

'Back door.'

'Right.' Girl checks her watch. 'Seven o'clock now. Two hours to kill.' She looks at Raj, smiles as cute as she knows how. 'Let's all go for cocktails somewhere?' Stops herself. Shit! She hasn't got any money.

'I'll pay.' Louise waves her purse at them. 'I know your grand-dad's dying so you must be short.'

Billy and Girl didn't hear that. It's just too damn risky to have heard that. Better to run with the plan. Action. Louise is fucking dangerous. Louise knows stuff and she's not letting on. Louise who goes with Danny the dog prince. Perhaps he is a wolf. Perhaps at midnight they both become wolves and howl in gardens all over north London. Making their way to Harkham Road. Making their way in the dead of night to eat the English chickens in their sleep.

13

'There he is.' Louise sits in the front seat of the Merc. Pointing at a figure locking a door. A man, wearing a raincoat, his leather briefcase between his knees. Two letters engraved on the lock. TT. Terry Tens.

Billy and Girl watch him. Their leading man. Notes have already been passed between them. Strategy. Military planning. Girl pokes Louise, her cue to get out of the car and walk towards Mr Tens. She's got to engage him in conversation while Billy and Girl creep up behind him. Meanwhile Raj is manoeuvring the Merc as close as he can get. The gears are playing up. First and reverse keep getting stuck, mixing into each other. When Raj wants to go forwards, he goes backwards. Nothing but a map of Girl's blond body in his mind as he tries to coax the fucking gear stick into some version of sane driving. Okay. Here goes.

Louise gets out of the car, walks towards her boss. 'Hello, Mr Tens.'

He jumps, frightened. Eyelashes fluttering in fear waves.

'It's only me. Left something in my locker.'

Mr Tens sighs. Shaking his head. Walking towards her. 'Can't it wait till tomorrow?'

'Yeah. I suppose so. What you got in your case?'

'Paperwork. Some of us never clock off, Louise.'

'Yeah? I just wanted to take my overall home to wash.'

Mr Tens looks at her, surprised and pleased. 'Glad to see you taking pride in your work. That really has made my day.'

Louise smiles at him, all the while watching Billy and Girl

sneak up behind Mr Tens, who seems to be in evangelical mode. It's like he thinks he's saved Louise from something. A fallen star that he caught in his upturned palm, just on the edge of his starched white shirt cuffs, ironed lovingly by his mother every Wednesday. Billy and Girl are getting closer. Wearing their trainers. No squelching, nothing. Raj opening the boot of the Merc, thinking about how the England kids are like movie stars, writing their own scripts but stalking their prey like any two-bit actors on the telly who have learnt how to do this from other actors on the telly.

'I'll walk you to the bus stop if you like, Louise. I go in the same direction.'

'Yeah?' Louise has never been one for long conversations.

Raj shakes his head. They're just so cute, these kids. Yeah, here they go. Billy throws himself behind Tens while Girl puts her hand over his mouth. Just his rainmac sleeves floundering this way and that. Louise picks up his briefcase. Walks over to the Merc and throws it in the boot. Billy has got his shoulder across Tens's chest now, lifting him up, he's not a heavy man. In fact Mr Tens is really light. Weighs in somewhere between a pack of frozen cod cutlets and a hormonal turkey thigh. Yeah, he's wizard Oz, this Mr Tens, got visions bigger than his bodily form, a small short man who wears very clean shirts. Tens is shouting something. 'LOoeeshe LOEESHE loueeshe' muffled behind Girl's hand, which is now a fist right inside his mouth, and he doesn't even think to bite her. Just yelling, 'Loueeeshe Loooeeshe.' Billy can almost run with Mr Tens over his shoulder. He could do a ten-mile hike with Tens sitting on his head. Dumps him in the boot while Raj bangs the door down, working out the complicated locking system. They all get back into the car, just not believing how easy this has been, and Girl starts mixing a manhattan from the minibar. Drinks all round. Cheers, pals!

Billy still not talking. Just grinning. Gulping back his drink. Yeah, Mom is very near. As far as Billy is concerned he's about to be more than all right. In Mom's lap. He's forgotten he's fifteen. Mom will make him a lickle bowl of soup and he'll fall asleep on her ample bosom while she strokes his cheek. Louise is withdrawn. In fact she looks downright unhappy. Girl resolves to bring her out of herself. Squeeze a better, braver Louise out of this one. Raj saying something about how the gears are fucked. Trying to get Billy to speak. 'Come on, Billy man, you can't be mute at a time like this.' Billy shakes his head. Nope. Won't even open his mouth to shout when Raj jerks the car right into an articulated lorry behind him, smashing the boot of the Merc. Puts his foot down before some big bloke pounds his way out of the lorry with 'LOVE HA HA' written on his forehead. Respectable speed on this Merc. Raj is in his element. Did a good job on the car. The future is bright. Fast car and a glamourous mad girl to keep happy.

Louise puts her sweet small hands over her mouth and Girl is guffawing because the only sound in the whole damn car is Mr Tens singing 'Onward Christian Soldiers'.

'Keep your pecker up, Mr Tens!' she screams, knocking back her minibar samples one by one, unscrewing the lids off miniatures and pouring them down her throat. Raj and Girl sing along while Billy claps his hands in time. Should have brought along his guitar. One day he will be as big as Jesus. He'll save people's souls and what's more he'll do it without a beard.

> 'Onward Christian soldiers
> marching on to war
> dum dum dum da da da.
> DUM DUM DUM DA DA DA
> DUM DUM DUM DA DA DA . . .'

14

Mr Tens is lying flat on his back on Girl's bed while Billy ties up his hands with one of Mom's scarves. Yeah. The clothes in Mom's wardrobe were going to come in useful one day. Billy often takes down the yellow dress, the one with the hem coming down, and sobs into it. A dress so hideous, it was designed for crying in, not partying in, Girl always says. Mr Tens bound like one of his FreezerWorld piglets. Little squeals twisting his lips. Prayers.

Billy sits on Tens's chest. Got a piece of paper on his lap and he's writing a note. MR TENS. YOU ARE GOD'S FREE GIFT TO US, THE SATURDAY BARGAIN. TELL US WHERE OUR MOTHER IS AND WE LET YOU GO.

Mr Tens shaking his head. Complete incomprehension. Billy's pen moving across the page again.

IF YOU DON'T TELL US WE'LL CUT YOUR TONGUE OFFFFFF. To help Tens make up his mind there's a little drawing of a severed tongue at the bottom of the page. Little drops of blood gushing all over. Raj has nipped out to get some teabags from the shop. They're all thirsty after Girl's miniature minibar molotovs.

'Yeah, Mr Tens,' Louise suddenly pipes up. She's been lurking in the room, crouching by the bed. 'We'll cut off your head and mince it.' A knife suddenly springs up between her thumb and fingers. That really makes Tens scream. Girl has to whack her fist into his mouth again. Blood on her fingernails from last time. Jeezuz. The bloke must have gingivitis. Vulnerable gums. Sensitive teeth. He must have to use a toothpaste with

160

something special in it. Not to mention the toothbrush. Soft bristles. Louise with a knife? Jeeeeeezuz. The girl's dangerous. A live wire. Billy catches the fear in Girl's eyes. All they need right now is a Louise explosion.

'Yeah, Mr Tens.' Louise stands up. 'We really will cut your tongue off.'

Billy nods, agreeing with everything Louise says always for ever etc. Rolls up his sleeves. Mr Tens watching. Trembling under the boy Billy. Girl knows she's got to keep out of this. Louise with a knife? Oh no. No no no no. Girl knows they've got to be careful with Louise. That's because Girl knows she's got to be careful with her secret Louise girl self. Not a knife. Oh no. Not with all that retard rage waiting for expression. She can hear the door slam downstairs. Raj coming in with the tea. Boiling the kettle. Billy doing something clever. Takes the knife off Louise. Sinks it into his wrist on behalf of Louise's rage. One clean cut.

His mom's only son, taking a little of Louise's rage on for her, that's the sort of person Billy is. Giving the knife back to Louise because that's the safest thing to do. He prefers working with his own knife anyway. Billy showing every little detail of his butchery to Mr Tens, whose pupils are spreading all over his eyes. Just blackness now. Especially now, because something has happened to Billy. He is sitting on top of Mr Tens just like his dad sat on top of him, five years old, teaching him how to box.

Except Dad has pinned down Billy's fists. Smacking Billy in the mouth, saying 'Let's see your left paw, son.' Bashing him and holding down his little body at the same time. Billy lets rip on Mr Tens. Whacking his fifteen-year-old fists into Tens's pale cheekbones. Slicing him with the side of his hand. Jagger jagger jagger. Bouncing on top of his breathing apparatus, bashing him and, worst of all, thinking it through at the same time. Billy's fists and Billy's mind working together. Bruising the pathetic Tens jaw, because he can. There are no safety regulations in this fight, just Billy bashing Dad, cos he's sitting on top of him and even though Mr Tens is not Dad, he'll do. Mr Tens trying to get words out of his mouth which is stuffed with Girl's white-trash fist.

'Want to say something?' Girl asks politely.

Tens nodding with his new blackness eyes.

'Go on then.'

Girl removes her hand. Jeezus. Trust them to pick someone with dental problems. Blood all over her fingers again. Hope he uses a mouthwash tried and tested in laboratories in the industrial UK. Blood from Billy's cut too. Girl's not interested in blood at all. She just wants information from the gulping, stuttering FreezerWorld wizard.

'Wah wah wwwant ta ta heelp . . .'

'Ey? Spit it out, Mr Tens.' Louise leers in his face.

'Waaaaaaant to heeelp.'

The bedroom door flings open. Raj carrying a tray. Five mugs of tea. Grinning on account of telling a Stupid Club member to repatriate himself to another local corner shop.

'I made one for him.' Raj cocks his head (Billy notices that Raj has found time to brush his hair) towards the bruised and squirming Tens. Raj is deeply shocked at the sight of Mr Tens. There's a new texture in his voice, a no-go zone. Raj is going to exit if they don't get a grip. 'Leave him alone.'

Girl nods obligingly, but she's ready to slam her fist back into the gingivitis man all the same.

'Wah wah wwwant to help the dddumb boy.' At last! Tens has made a sentence. Everyone's laughing except Billy. Hey, Mr Tens, you really have a way with words that will make you friends and influence people. The Dumb Boy.

'Go on, then. How you gonna make him talk?' Girl prods

162

the hostage while Louise takes her teaspoon, dips it into the tea and feeds it to Mr Tens like soup. That's what her mother did for her. When she was cold, all snot and filth and no sleep.

'I'm a bb bah bah bbbit of a healer.' Is Tens trying to save his penis? What, for Mr Tens? For FreezerWorld? For FreezerWoman?

'Do it then. Heal the wounded.' Raj is acting cool but he's also sincere. A little bit of Raj believes Mr Tens's healing claim. You got to believe and then lose it, don't you? Or get sad and then find faith? That's how life on earth works. You make a judgement and then you correct it. Raj wants to hear his friend Billy whine again.

'La la la look at the space between mah mah mah my eyebrows, Bahbbilly.'

Billy sitting on Mr Tens the bruised breathless healer. All his boy weight pressing down on the man. Complete concentration. This is a tremulous moment in the life of Billy England. He wants a bigger audience. Girl, Louise, Raj. That's only three. Billy wants some noughts at the end of that number. Choosing the spot between the eyebrows. Focus there. Beam in his pain biography to that place. Send it to Mr Tens unadulterated. Don't clean it up. Send it dirty like it is. Breathe in and shoot out a pain laser that contains everything Billy England is, right between the healer's eyes.

Go.

Raj finds his knuckles are in his mouth. Girl is chewing the ends of her hair. Louise sipping her tea. Billy is completely still and silent but Mr Tens is writhing. Sweat dripping from his eyebrows into his bleeding mouth. Gasping. 'GahGahGah . . .'

Time for Louise to spoon more tea into her boss's mouth. After all, he does pay her her wages in a little brown envelope every Friday. Mustn't upset him too much.

'Gah gah gah.'

Girl is getting restless. 'Come on, Mr Tens. You're the one supposed to make my brother talk. Not doing so well yourself.'

Mr Tens suddenly sits bolt upright, throwing Billy off him, warm sugary tea dribbling out of his trembling lips. 'Gah gah ded!' he howls. 'Gah ded.'

Billy scrambling to get up. Thrown onto his stomach, caught in the fringe of the rug in Girl's room. A caveboy struggling with faith, the elements and the shame of beating Mr Tens. He thought he was above that. What with his books and scholarship. Trying to find his pen and paper.

Raj is genuinely worried. 'Why did you have to go and do that to the man?' he whispers, taking a pencil from his jeans pocket, nervous when his friend grabs it and starts writing furiously, all the while Louise stroking Mr Tens's forehead. It's like her boss is in labour. Gah Gah ded contractions every minute. Crying out.

RAJ I aM THe ONly HEALER IN THIS ROOM. UNDERSTAND?

Raj reading the Billy note, nodding just to be on the safe side but he doesn't have comprehension of anything any more. Billy crossing out stuff, writing more. Girl can't be bothered to wait for her brother.

'Look, Mr Tens. You make announcements in FreezerWorld, don't you?'

Vigorous nodding from the gibbering hostage.

'Right. One of the announcements said, "Louise call Grand-Dad. If his horse hasn't come home he might be ill."'

Tens choking now, but still nodding.

'Who gave you that note to announce, Mr Tens?'

Louise pouring tea into her boss's mouth. He's stopped shaking. In fact his pale face is beginning to tan. Some kind of sunlight whispering through Tens, despite the choking and howling. He is a man who has been penetrated by a fifteen-year-old boy. Penetrated by revelation. He can only describe it (and he will, if he lives to make another FreezerWorld broadcast) as a rock cracking under an immense lonely sky. Between the two halves of rock is just space. Tens has entered that space. Emptied of God belief but fattened with belief all the same. A mortal man touched, literally, with the pain of a mortal boy. The boy is the carrier of the pain, but Tens knows that it is a paincrowd that touched him. Mothers and fathers and government policies and vitamin lack and self-taught languages and menthol inhalings. There was even an Alsatian dog present in the pain glare that blitzed him between the eyes and nudged God out of his solar system. Recipes and technologies and highway codes. He has been penetrated by castration theories and pain ash, lager longing and boy autonomy insistence; there is even a road in Nottingham grazing Tens's third-eye space, plus pepperoni-pizza enlightenment and silver loafers and sentiment leaking, crashing into each other. Tens is fighting through a Looney Tune vortex with 'That's all folks' flashing on and off, soundbites from Freud and Darwin and Jackie Collins. Tens is a changed man. Godless but full up all the same.

'Yes.' Mr Tens speaks with clarity and confidence. 'Someone did give me a note to read.' He looks at Louise and smiles gently. 'Mrs O'Reilly.'

Girl kicks the bed. 'Who the fuck is Mrs O'Reilly?'

It's Louise's turn now. Plaiting her blond hair. Sitting close to Mr Tens. 'My mother.'

'That's right, Louise.' Mr Tens has found his voice again.

'Don't talk to me like that.' Louise pounces on her boss. Tearing at his little bow tie like it's his intestines.

'How do you want me to talk to you, Louise?' The hostage man floundering again. Finding his way and then losing it almost immediately.

'I work for my shit money. There's plenty more shit out there for me to get up in the morning for so don't come on like you're giving me free air miles, Captain fucking Tens!'

'Mrs O'Reilly?' Girl has changed tactics. She's threatening Louise. 'Come on, who is she?'

'Mrs O'Reilly took Louise in,' Tens explains. Yes. He's been missing his FreezerWorld Broadcasting. Mr Tens has become addicted to an audience. Even here, when he should be somewhere else, somewhere safer, more familiar, he's pleased to have knowledge he can share. Somewhere inside, he knows he's going to be all right. 'Louise ran away from home and Mrs O'Reilly was kind enough to take her in.'

Louise has made two perfect plaits out of her blondness. Pinning them up with her new plastic heart hair slides. Her horror eyes flirt with Girl. Nearly there. One more tug with the hairgrip. 'She got me the job at FreezerWorld.'

Billy is putting on his jacket. Tying up his trainer laces. Pulling a comb through his hair. Wrapping his shirt sleeve tight over his new cut. Nothing serious. Preparing himself. He looks at Girl and she nods. Pale and cold.

'Get *up!*' She yanks Mr Tens off the bed. 'Take us to Mrs O'Reilly, then. Get up now!'

Raj is already dangling the Merc keys, ready to drive Girl and Billy anywhere they want to go. He wants the Englands to be happy and safe. He wants them to be all right. And Louise too. Thing is, Louise and Tens have some weird complicity. They're like a sort of family. Hating and loving each other.

'My mother works nights sometimes.' Louise says meekly, but her eyes are snared with Girl. Taunting her.

That's just too much for Girl. She doesn't care what Raj thinks of her any more. She leaps on Louise. Wrestles her to the floor. Pulls her hair and punches her face. Billy holding off Mr Tens who wants to rescue Louise princess. No fucking way, Mr Tens. Girl is a princess too. Billy knows that. He always tells his sister so. Forget this Evil thing. That's for Stupid Club. That's for medievalists on buses all over the city. In their mixed fibres and High Street shoes shouting Evil Evil Evil cos it's easier than shouting Pain Pain Pain. Fifteen minutes of medieval fame. Girl is a princess too. A princess for the twenty-first.

'Where is she where is she *where is she?*' Girl scrunches Louise's cheeks in her hands, pulling them apart, biting her. Girl teeth marks in Louise. Girl yanking out Louise hair, Girl nails stuck in Louise flesh, but Louise won't so much as flinch. Not even a tear. Louise, Princess of FreezerWorld. Packing peas for ever. 4 Ever. That's how the Louise story goes. She did not live happily for ever after. She lived happily 4 ever after. Louise pulls out her knife.

'Come and get me then, Louise,' she whispers to Girl. Calling her Louise for the first time. 'Come and fucking get me. I saw you stalking me. Following me home. Finding excuses to stare at me at work . . . what do you want to *do* with me then, Louise?'

Louise. A princess for the twenty-first, armed and alert. Threats spilling from her soft cupid lips, rage in her white girl curves and dainty bitten off nails.

'Calling me stunted. Calling me retard. Calling my boyfriend a dog. Come and get me then.'

Girl backs away. Pushes her face against the wallpaper of her girlhood bedroom. Louise walks her eyes around the details of Girl's girl room. Fixes them on Billy who is writing again. He's writing for Girl's life. Got to take maternal care of Girl. What Mom should have done, stopped Dad pulping her boy, Girl did. Burnt her very own prince. The first prince in her life. Can't have a prince that beats up the next heir to the throne, can you? Not good for the kingdom. The orchards rot. Locusts eat the national crop. The water becomes polluted. Billy is a boy with an unspoken message from Mom inside him: Look after Girl.

Girl disappearing into the faded teddy-bear wallpaper, shrinking from Louise's gaze, dazzled by its loopy intensity, burying her head in the faint outline of one of the pastel-coloured teddies' big swollen belly. A stomach just like an infant's, but smooth, without a navel where the cord was cut at birth, knotted and bleeding, a little stump to be powdered.

Crying into the bear's small round ears, wetting the paper with her Girl tears, spontaneous catastrophic tears which she will have to give up one day and replace with stoic adult tears, like she will have to give up this bedroom and her plastic bubble bath creatures and soaps in the shape of hippos and dolphins.

'You and me and the clothes and that—' Louise pointing her knife in Girl's direction – 'what's it all for?'

Girl says, 'You were just girlmeat when I first saw you. Packing peas in your sad shoes. Girlmeat, no label, no frills. EEC: thaw before cooking. What a disgusting sight. I made you into a better brand of Louise to cheer myself up.'

'Yeah?' FreezerWorld Louise pretending she's thinking about this, tapping the knife against her teeth. In a minute she's going to smash the blade right through Girl's head. 'Wetard Wetard Wetard Wetard.' Louise makes her way towards Girl, half screaming, half whispering, 'Wetard Wetard Wetard Wetard, I'm a WEeeeTAaaaaRD,' stretching her lips to make 'WEEEEEEEeeeeetAAAAAaaaaaard' last for ever, slamming her knife into one of the wallpaper teddies, ripping out its awed round eyes. 'Weetaaaaard weetaaaard weetaaaard weetaaaard weetaaaard weetaaaard weetaaaard weetaaaard weetaaaard weetaaaard.' Squeaking her voice, 'Weetaaaaaard weeeeeetard weeeeeeeeeeeeetard weeeeeeeeeeeeetard,' carving at the wallpaper, scratching LOUISE in the plaster with the point of her knife. Stumbling towards the dressing table, slashing at the child princess's furniture bought by Dad when Girl was seven, an old-fashioned one with a mirror and little drawers. Secret places to hide a girl diary, under the pink polka-dot girl socks with Girl's secret name sewn inside, 'Louise' looped in blood-red daisy stitch.

Girl knows that Louise wants to carve her secret name into her girl flesh, coming at her to brand the first L into her cheek. The Louise snarl-up. Is that what it takes to give up Girl? Blood? Billy gives his note to Raj. Gesturing him to read it out loud. Raj licking his lips, which feel like bone. Heart pounding under the new shirt at the sight of his girlfriend sobbing and FreezerWorld Louise becoming the thing she was called, showing them just how good she can *do* retard.

TO GIRLS EVERY WHERE. RAJ AND BILLY ARE THE GODS OF LOVE AND LAGER. WE ARE READY TO ENJOY LIFE WITH GIRLS. THE MALE CITIZENS OF TWENTY FIRST. GOOD LOOKING, GOT THE WORDS, WELL HUNG, WILL rISK proMotiON pROSPECTS to DEFEND the righTS of GIRLS WE LOVE. WE ARE fUtUre MAN. DEaTH TO OLD KIND OF DAD PRINCE—

Mr Tens interrupts Raj. He's even plucked up enough courage to shout and whirl his bow tie. 'Shut up, Raj! You're giving me a fucking migraine.'

Louise folds her arms, knife loose in her hand. 'Yeah. Shut the fuck up too, Billy! I was having a conversation with your sister. 'Snot me who's girlmeat, you stoopid cunt, why dyuthink I ran away then? Start taking notes, Billy . . . Go on . . . Fuck you, Billy, let's see that pen move or I'll kill your sister.'

Billy does what he's told.

'Sometimes you got to make a run for it, dontcha? Weeeeeeetard weeeeeeetard . . . write it Billy, write Weeeeeeetard Weeetard weeetard for ever and ever write it for ever and ever weeeeeeeeeeeeeeeeeeeeeetard write it in your book, Billy,

169

weeeeeeeeeeeeeeeeeeeetard, she's com-ing to get you, weeeetard's coming to get you, here comes weeeeeeeeeeeeeeeeeeeeeeeeeeetard.' She makes her way towards Girl, whose dirty blond ponytail is falling out of the plastic heart grip, same as the one she bought Louise, tripping over a child's pair of blue plastic sandals neatly lined up under the dressing table that has been ruined for ever. 'I knew who you was before you even clapped eyes on me,' FreezerWorld Louise is whispering now. Measuring her words. Making the brother and sister lean forward to hear her. She takes out a little pot of lip gloss with a picture of a kiwi fruit on the lid. Dips her chewed-up finger into the green balm and smears it on her lips. 'Seen photos of you at Mrs O'Reilly's. And *you*, Billy fucking England.'

She pauses, screwing up her eyes, little flesh furrows on her see-thru skin.

'Mrs O'Reilly's in FreezerWorld tonight.' Louise throws the knife on the floor.

'Thing is, I don't think your mother wants to see you.'

15

The Merc is a nerve bomb. Nerve atoms jumping into the purple velveteen seats. Working their way into Merc metal and glass.

Billy, Mr Tens and Louise in the back. Raj and Girl in the front. Billy and Louise both holding knives where healer Tens can see them.

No cocktails this time. Raj keeping his eye on the road. He feels Merc weirdness seeping into his hands from the steering wheel. Mrs O'Reilly? Hasn't he met her? The woman who came to see the car. Fingering the upholstery, as if she knew every curve of the metal beneath it. Walking around the Merc wreck like it was a house she used to live in. He looks at his watch.

'Five to eleven.' Raj doesn't know why he said this. I mean, who wants to know?

North London streets. A few kebab shops open. Dry cleaners offering a special price on duvets. Blokes with cans sitting in shop doorways. Crap shops like Raj's father's crap shop. Shops selling nylon mittens, outsize brassieres, crap bath mats, dog biscuits shaped like baby boots and bones, crap carpet shops and crap betting shops. The crap chemists and their bored indifferent pharmacists frowning over prescriptions all year round, handing out pills and syrups to citizens with symptoms. The crap shop on the left that sells yams and plantains, right next to the crap shop that sells crap curtains and wallpaper for all the English houses and conversions and flats. What kind of life is he, Raj, going to make for himself? Yeah, it's true he likes a kebab sometimes. Maybe one day he'll buy the family dog a stinking baby's-boot bone with Xtra iron in it. Maybe one day he'll buy a bath mat from one of the crap shops. Many a time he's swallowed cough elixir bought from a crap chemist. Sipping the pink stuff from a five-ml plastic spoon.

Silence from Master England. Got nothing to say. Funny sort of a doctor he's turned out to be. Goes dumb just when Raj actually needs his words for a change. Look at the teenage quack biting his tongue, sitting there motionless, dead still, like there's a killer wasp hovering above his head. Just his little knife and pain index, going through it in his head, A to Z.

Girl's got other things on her mind. 'Front or back entrance?'

'Back,' Mr Tens, hostage, a man who lost his God faith with one Billy glare, replies happily and calmly. He's enjoying the ride.

FreezerWorld at night. Everything is milky blue. Ivory and pearl. A world without stars. The Frozen World. Rumbling of fridges across the ice fields. Dome of white sky. Long solitary journeys across the frozen ocean aisles. Mr Tens. An Arctic Marco Polo who knows the cartography of FreezerWorld with his eyes shut.

Raj feels the cold freeze the marrow of his bones. It's as if he can hear a seal barking in the distance, which is far away, a confusion of whites and greys. Musk oxen and hares disappearing into the snow. Somewhere, near the frozen-fish section, the ivory-white head of a polar bear searches for her cubs. Raj knows that she is Billy and Girl's mother. Grey tongue. Purple mouth. White teeth. Hissing as she prowls the ice fields. The ice bear, creature of the Arctic edges, listening out for clues.

She dives into the ocean, takes a deep long breath, plunges under and walks the sea beds searching for mussels and kelp. Dragging slabs of meat from a beached whale, calling out to her cubs to come and feast. Large silent feet checking for ice cracks and explosions of sea ice. Opening FreezerWorld tins with the rake of a claw. Searching for tundra berries in the snax section. On her hind legs piercing a battery-hen egg and sucking it dry. Drawing breath without sound. Under the neon night light her fur is a collection of whites, apricot yellows, straw, ripe wheat. Frolicking. Juggling packets of mustard pretzels in her paws. Sleeping with her eyes open, ears twitching.

Mr Tens is master of the Frozen World. Assured now. Walking with confidence through the ice maze, no Muzak, taking special care of Louise because she is on his payroll. One of his fisherwomen. Treading quietly, finger on his lips, 'I don't want to scare her.'

Her. Billy and Girl can't believe he says 'her' so breezily. Stops outside a door with his name on it. MR TENS, MANAGER. Gestures for them to wait while he knocks on his own door. Turns the handle. Peers in.

'Only me, Mrs O'Reilly.'

A woman's voice saying something. 'Hello, Terry. Nearly finished the script for Monday.' Terry Tens putting his face in.

Mrs O'Reilly reading her script, not looking at him. No expression in her voice. She sounds tired.

'Good morning, ladies and gentlemen. And thank you for starting your week at FreezerWorld. Today we're proud to offer you quality goods for every budget.' She stops. Weary. 'Just the usual, Terry. I mentioned the reduction on yesterday's bread. And an announcement for Louise if you don't mind. To call the hospital for news of her grandfather. Can you read my writing?'

Mr Tens stands to one side as Girl, Billy, Louise and Raj walk into his secret FreezerWorld life.

Mrs O' Reilly sits at a desk surrounded with sheets of paper. Writing by hand. Scripts written and crossed out. Just like Billy's recent notes. Shoes neatly tucked under her chair. A plate of FreezerWorld lemon fingers placed just so by her mug of tea. Red hundred per cent wool coat hanging on a hook behind the door.

Mom. A room of her own in the superstore. Earning her keep in the FreezerWorld. Writing words for Mr Tens to broadcast. Writing messages to her kiddies. The security cameras hidden in the managerial office warned her in advance that the hunting party were trudging towards her. She watched them climb through the corridors of FreezerWorld stock waiting to be unpacked. Her children on the screen walking through the Frozen World to claim their frozen mother. Hunters with tension in their bodies, alert, hungry and fearful. Mrs O'Reilly willing them to stop in their tracks and turn back, checking the screen to see if they carry hunting weapons. Following her scent. Mom. A creature of the Arctic edges. Hibernating, nocturnal, terrified.

Mom looking so ordinary. Bit of a new hairstyle. Faint circles under her eyes. Sitting there staring at them all. Billy and Girl and Louise with blood on their clothes. The two girls look the worst. Like they've thrown themselves into the propeller of a small helicopter. Perhaps she should take them all straight to casualty? That way she won't have to say anything for a while. Just give them to doctors and nurses, fill in forms, hold their hands while their cuts and bruises are dabbed with antiseptic, stitched and bandaged up, making conversation with the receptionist about the weather. It's a bit rainy, if you know what I mean. Not exactly rain. More like slabs of frozen sea. Treading water between the cracks.

There they are. Her kiddies. Not even the security video could prepare her for how much they've changed. She bought them a card for every one of their five birthdays without her and never sent them. What are Mom's first words?

'How are you, Rajindra?'

Raj goes mad. Loops his thumbs into his belt and starts ranting. 'I'm not all right, Mrs O'Reilly. I'm done in.' Walks across the FreezerWorld managerial carpet, waving his arms. 'Done everything I can for your fucking mad, demented children. Mended their crap car, fed'em the crap food they like, minding my own business in my own crap shop and then I do what boys do and kiss a girl.' Sly look at Louise and Louise. 'What happens, your fucking son goes crazy on me. Won't talk. I mean, what's wrong with him, what's wrong with her, it's what people do, they kiss each other, you know, it's hormones, romance, it's an old idea, you've seen it on TV, you've seen it at fucking bus stops, you've seen it on chocolate wrappers, you've seen it on bottles of nail-varnish remover, you see it all the time, right?' Raj making his way towards his girlfriend's brother. 'What did I do to make you go dumb, you stoopid fucker . . . I put my lips like this—' Raj puts his arm around Billy, presses his lips against his boy lips and sticks his tongue into Billy's boy mouth. 'That's what it is, it's called kissing . . .' Billy shoves his fist straight into Raj's nose . . . knocks him flat out cold on the FreezerWorld liver-pâté-coloured carpet.

'What do you think you're doing, Billy?' Mrs O'Reilly stands up, brushing crumbs off her neat blue dress. 'No son of mine cracks a punch at someone who shows them a bit of affection!'

She makes her way to Raj in her tan tights, kneels down and wipes his forehead with a little tea towel. 'I'm disgusted,' Mrs O'Reilly says again. 'Hitting out like that.'

Stroking Raj's hair. Cooing at him. Rajindra? Saying 'Rajindra' over and over like the tape has got stuck, looking at her kids and Mr Tens too. Has Terry been fighting? Looks like he's been in a pub brawl.

'When he kissed me everything went yellow,' Billy says, clutching his chin, holding his arms out towards Mom. Louise and Girl biting their hands, not wanting to put Billy off his first words. Billy is a baby and he's just got language. Put his first sentence together. Little squeaky voice.

'Everything went yellow.' Girl knows Billy's talking about what it felt like to be slugged by Dad when he was five.

Such a long way to Mom, falling on to her, no kiss, just arms around her, eyes shut, and Girl walking in that direction now, shy steps, taking it slowly, Mom holding out one of her arms. Girl making her way there.

'Dear,' Mom says. Dear. Such an old word. From her heart to her lips. Mom's love word just swiped them on the cheek and moistened them with tears. It was as if she had said 'Beloved', crammed all the meaning of 'beloved' into 'dear' because she was too shy to say anything grandiose or flamboyant. Keeping it simple, stating obvious things, no speech up her sleeve to cry through.

Mrs O'Reilly looks up at FreezerWorld Louise. The girl she took in because she had the same name as her daughter. Loving her. 'What are those bruises on your face?'

Louise is not shy, walking fast towards her mother.

'How did you get to be in such a mess?' Mom staring at her two girls, fighting to free her hand under Billy who won't budge. 'What happened to your face?'

FreezerWorld Louise says, 'Sorting it out. Lou and me. It's okay.'

'I'm glad to hear it.'

Raj opens his eyes. Everyone on the floor with him. Mom and Girl and Louise and Billy. All in a huddle on their knees. Mr Tens eating the lemon fingers. 'Gah gah gah gah gah ded ded gah gah ded.'

'What have you done to him?' Mrs O'Reilly whispering.

Billy stirring. Breathing easier. 'He's saying god's dedd. Wants a pizza.'

'Why's he saying that, Billy?'

FreezerWorld Louise is sitting with her mother. Waiting for everyone. Mom smearing a little bit of Nivea into her cheeks. They really went for each other, those girls.

'Billy's a bit of a doctor,' FreezerWorld Louise says.

'Is that right?' Mrs O'Reilly is interested.

'Yeah. He's writing a book on pain.'

Mr Tens is gargling with mouthwash. Listening in. 'What's it called, Billy?' Terry Tens spitting out FreezerWorld's own brand for tender gums.

''S called *Billy England's Book of Pain*.'

Billy doing up his trainer laces. Mom combing through Girl's hair with her fingers. Louise washing her face in the little managerial basin in the corner. Stainless-steel taps. Soaping her hands with the nice FreezerWorld soap. Smelling it. Rose petal and geranium. Bringing it to Mom to smell. All of them still waiting for Billy's answer because Mr Tens is gibbering, gargling, licking the lemon icing off the plate.

Mrs O'Reilly smiling at her boy and his pizza pangs. 'Go on, Girl, wash your face too.'

'Louise,' Girl says. 'My fucking name is Louise.'

'Louise.' Mom nods. Looks around her. They all look so tired.

177

Worn out. Exhausted. Blood spots on their clothes. Bruised. Billy's put his arm round his sister.

'My name is Louise. My fucking name is Louise.'

Billy murmuring something to Mom. Crazy for his mother. 'Good thing Girl's mad, otherwise I wouldn't have had a patient to practise on at such a young age.'

'She's called Louise.' Mrs O'Reilly stands up. 'And she's not mad. We got to sort ourselves out.' Makes her way to the neatly arranged shoes under the chair. Slips them on. Walks to the table, picks up her script, reads it through, puts a line across a few sentences. Reads it through again. 'That's ready to go for Monday, Terry,' she says with a note of stern last-draft finality in her voice.

Mrs O'Reilly feels something rushing at her. Stinging her. It's joy. Like an Arctic wind burning up everything that isn't here, her kiddies, with her, in the present time.

'Mom?' Billy asking her a question.

'Dear?'

'Why didn't you stop Dad pulping me?'

Mrs O'Reilly. Suddenly the wind chills and freezes the tips of her ears. Tips of her fingers. Crashes into her cheekbones. Bruises every vertebra of her spine. Her lips taste of salt and blood. Arcs of ice crystals cover her eyebrows. Ice and light and space and the bottom of the world melting so there's nowhere to put her tan nylon feet, nowhere to flee from her hunters.

'Terry. I think you should take out the second "and" in Monday's broadcast. Just run the words together.'

'Uh?'

Billy looking dangerous now. 'Say why.'

'Yes, I will,' says Mrs O'Reilly. But she doesn't. She just stands there. Silent. What's Mom thinking about? Grand-Dad who died three weeks ago? Her father buried under the wreath she ordered from the florists? Lilies and roses for her father.

'Graham England Rest in Peace.' Anything for a bit of peace and rest.

FreezerWorld Louise helps her out. Dearness in her voice. Sort of whispering because they met each other when they both needed love and they help each other out.

'He's saying ... wants to know why you didn't protect him.'

The FreezerWorld wind is a crisis wind. Frostbite and trackers baiting their steel traps.

Mrs O'Reilly. Numbness is pain turned inside out. Wearing her cardigan the wrong way round. 'It was my beehive, Billy.' She smiles through the wind and silent falling snow. How many words are there for snow? For pain, poverty, love, regret, knowing how to say the right thing at the right moment, for little vests with poppers between the legs and fingers of fish and No Tears Shampoo?

'Was a very difficult hairstyle to get perfect. Took such a long time to get it right. The teasing and lacquer. All those pins. Combing out the fringe. Pleating in all those little stray bits. Folding and tucking.'

Billy lunges at her. Knocks her to the ground. Kill her Kill her Kill her. Dump her in the FreezerWorld freezers. Taking out his knife.

'Say why.'

'I was very proud of my hair . . .'

'Why didn't you stop him?'

Mrs O'Reilly shaking her head at Billy's knife. 'Say why for me in your pain book.'

Billy thinking about this. Rubbing the lobe of his left ear between his fingers. Scratching the back of his hands. Digging his front teeth into his bottom lip. Fluttering his eyelids and making them still again. Curling his toes up tight, straightening them, doing that three times, a boy full of tics and twitches.

Something to think about on a rainy day when he's got a bit of time on his hands.

'Why should I?'

FreezerWorld Louise interrupts. 'Because you can.'

'Yeah.'

Although Billy says 'yeah' his voice is cold. Blank. Yeah, he can. So what? Worth being born for, is it? That's all right then, is it? Being all right. Being brave. Being okay. What kind of Being is that? Being clever, does that make it all right then? Is it all right being in a concentration camp cos you might live to write about it afterwards? Live through it again so other people get the gist, and then top yourself – probably before your bloody royalty cheque comes through? What is a man? What is an ashtray? Naaaa. Better to go down the Leisure Centre and do trampolining. Write a book about how to perfect a triple backward somersault. Better to sell carpets and make your customers happy with a special deal for the underlay and fitting. Should have put a stop to her. Cut her throat there and then and chucked her into the fridges with BELOW ACCEPTABLE STANDARD labels on them.

Mrs O'Reilly manages to stand up. Her nose is bleeding and her daughters scrabble about to get her a tissue. A sad, angry smile on their faces, watching their mother stroking Billy's neck. Louise England giving Raj or Rajindra as her mother called him – how did she know his full name? – the tiniest kiss she can. She wants to kiss him tiny beginner's kisses. Holding his hand in her hand.

'Hi, Louise.' Raj grimaces.

'Hi, baby.'

'Will you ever be normal?' Raj's enquiry is really heartfelt, even though it's a sexy fuzzy whisper in her ear.

'Dunno, Rajindra.'

Raj ties back her peroxide hair for her with the elastic band she's just given him.

'Might be all right if I never have to ride in a minicab again.'

Billy, who is soaping his face with the lovely FreezerWorld rose-petal soap, interrupts. 'That's right, Raj. I never want my sister to ride in a minicab again. Understand?'

Raj checks out Billy under all that soap. Keep the boy talking. 'Will Louise . . . be all right, doc?'

'It's not "all right" we're after here, Raj.'

Raj sighs. Perhaps he shouldn't encourage the creep to talk after all. Not so much an answer as a tutorial.

'Pain has its own language. You got to listen in.'

'Are you ready?' Mrs O'Reilly calling out to everyone, soaping themselves, gargling, brushing their hair. No one is ready. For anything. Whatever 'ready' means.

'You're coming too.' Mrs O'Reilly tugs at Mr Tens's shoulder.

Billy and his sister glance at each other. Jeezus. Mom collects 'em like carrier bags, doesn't she? Mrs O'Reilly putting her arm round Louise and Louise. Raj and Mr Tens discussing the low points of running a business as they all troop downstairs towards the exit doors. Billy leading the way. FreezerWorld. A zone where the weather is always the same. A one-season Eden without sunrise and birdsong. Its children crying real tears for crisps and juices.

'To tell the truth, Mrs O'Reilly, I don't feel up to driving.'

Raj is resting his hand on the Merc roof. Leaning against the door. His arms feel weak. Tears are about to leak down his cheeks. Suddenly finds himself thinking about his little brother reading comics by the till. The Alsatian lying on a bit of old cardboard on the floor. His mother smiling politely at Stupid Club all day. His dad promising her a better life soon. What kind of a better life? His mum says she wants to try that happy drug. Get the prescription for her. 'Patel, Mrs Prozac. Take X times a day.' Raj interferes. Says, 'No way, Mum, I'll get you some crack instead. That will cheer you up. We can smoke it when Dad visits Uncle. Light up and watch repeats of the *Alan Partridge Show*.'

'I'll be driving tonight, if you don't mind, Raj?' Mrs O'Reilly gentling her voice.

Raj throws her the keys, turns his back on them all and wipes his eyes on his shirt cuffs. Someone once told him that if you find a single eyelash on your hand, make a wish. It's lucky. What should he wish for? Sometimes wishes are cumbersome things. Heaving into the universe when they should just spin . . . like a wish to make someone happy . . . wishes whispered with a heavy heart. Raj wishes his little brother the electric guitar he's been pining for. Yelping and pouting his rock-fame routine in front of the bathroom mirror while the whole family queue outside to brush their teeth. Preparing for another day of Stupid Club and rain.

Mrs O'Reilly stares in wonder at the purple interior of the Merc. 'You made it lovely, Raj,' she says, climbing in, giving orders as she turns the key and revs up. 'I want Billy and Louise and Raj in the back, and you in the front with me,' pointing to FreezerWorld Louise. She stops. 'Terry, you're going to have to go in the boot. It's not far, just a five-minute spin to Pizza Express.'

Terry Tens gibbering again. 'Peeza pe pe peeeza.' Louise straightening her boss's crooked bloodstained bow tie.

Mrs O'Reilly remembering something: 'Do you want me to pick up Danny on the way?'

'I'll see him tomorrow. Not enough room.'

Raj politely leads Mr Tens to the boot. 'Gently does it,' he says, helping Tens curl up in foetal position, covering him with a blanket, trying to keep a straight face because all the kids' shoulders are shaking.

'Gah Gah . . . peeeza peeeza peeza . . .'

FreezerWorld Louise begins to crack up. Mouth wide open, big girl laughter filling the Merc.

Mrs O'Reilly adjusts the mirror so she can keep an eye on her kids in the back. 'What's wrong with you all?'

Billy pressing his entire face against the window to stop Terry Tens's boot laughter exploding the Merc into tiny pieces of boiling metal. Louise and Raj folded into each other screaming hysterically. I mean, how many times in your life do you get to travel in a born-again Merc boot twice in one day? Both Louises spluttering, stopping, spluttering, giving in to complete abandon and howling.

'I dunno what's wrong with you lot.' Mrs O'Reilly reversing now. 'Don't you like pizza any more or something?'

'Mom.' Billy wipes the snot that's run into his mouth on the back of his hand. 'Why do you call yourself Mrs O'Reilly? You're Mrs England, aren't you?'

Mom shrugs, a bit shaky at the wheel, looking for something in her handbag and trying to steer at the same time. Still writing the words for Terry's broadcasts in her head. Got to find copy for the delivery of bratwurst on Monday. A new taste sensation to introduce into the lifestyle of the customer. Bratwurst must become as popular as chicken winglets.

'Suits me better.'

'Peeza peeza peeza peeza,' Tens bleating from the boot. Setting them all off again.

'Did you know your grand-dad died?'

No answer. They haven't even heard her.

'He's left us some money. The two-thirty came home.'

Billy and his sister can finish off each other's sentences without even discussing it. So the old clown's made them laugh at last. His horse came home! All those years ago when Louise England counted horses in fields on their car drives to Kent, she was secretly searching on Grand-Dad's behalf for *the* horse that was going to come home. Now they can learn how to be rich and unfocused. Have no motivation and become junkies. Christ thought he would heal them with his pain but Grand-Dad knew better and healed them with his gambling habit. Perhaps they will sell their pain story to the US chat shows after all? Yeah. Once they have sorted everything out like she . . . her . . . what's her name . . . Mum . . . Mom . . . like their mother says.

Billy hopes that when he sets up his practice, the first patient will be a good-looking blonde with breast enlargements and delusions. He will explain to her that a person who cannot experience pain is a freak. A sideshow wonder. Pricking, tingling, aching, tender, nagging, mild, excruciating.

Time for a weather check. It's pouring. Pelting down. Lashing on to the screen. The English weather. Why hasn't Mom put the wipers on? Naaa. Naaaaaa. Click on the wipers? She must know that would be like killing a dragon with a toy sword. Fighting off rage with an aspirin. Trying to save a drowning child by sailing out in a plastic tea cup. Billy's looking forward to his pizza. In fact he's not going to order a pizza at all. A change of diet to prepare himself for the can of worms he's going to open. Perhaps Raj's dad will take the photo for the back of his book cover? Looks like the old man's going to be an in-law, the way things are going. Smile, Billy! Smile, Bill-ee boy! Go on, it might never happen! Yeah. He's going to have Calzone. What's a Calzone? Just a pizza folded up, with a filling of his choice, isn't it? Tonight Billy's going to order a snail Calzone.

Mrs O'Reilly is a real petrol head. She loves being at the wheel, enjoying the feel of the car as she swerves to avoid a newer streamlined model of Mercedes trying to overtake her. She's found what she's been fumbling for in her bag, the FreezerWorld marker pen that's earned her a living and where she first spotted her kids. Looking down from Tens's office when Girl made her first purchase, an aerosol of red spray paint. MOM CALL HOME GIRL. It was right and proper that they all met up again in the Frozen World. Graffiti runs in the family. Quick as a flash she writes something in big letters across the windscreen. All of them leaning forward to see what the secret scriptwriter for Terry Tens has written in indelible ink on the Merc.

All the other cars beeping their hooters at the lights when they read the screen.

MOM AND HER BROOD.   /

SELECTED DALKEY ARCHIVE PAPERBACKS 🔲

YUZ ALESHKOVSKY, *Kangaroo.*
FELIPE ALFAU, *Chromos.*
    Locos.
DJUNA BARNES, *Ladies Almanack.*
    Ryder.
JOHN BARTH, *LETTERS.*
    Sabbatical.
ANDREI BITOV, *Pushkin House.*
ROGER BOYLAN, *Killoyle.*
CHRISTINE BROOKE-ROSE, *Amalgamemnon.*
GABRIELLE BURTON, *Heartbreak Hotel.*
MICHEL BUTOR, *Portrait of the Artist as a Young Ape.*
JULIETA CAMPOS, *The Fear of Losing Eurydice.*
ANNE CARSON, *Eros the Bittersweet.*
LOUIS-FERDINAND CÉLINE, *Castle to Castle.*
    London Bridge.
    North.
    Rigadoon.
HUGO CHARTERIS, *The Tide Is Right.*
JEROME CHARYN, *The Tar Baby.*
EMILY HOLMES COLEMAN, *The Shutter of Snow.*
ROBERT COOVER, *A Night at the Movies.*
STANLEY CRAWFORD, *Some Instructions to My Wife.*
RENÉ CREVEL, *Putting My Foot in It.*
RALPH CUSACK, *Cadenza.*
SUSAN DAITCH, *Storytown.*
PETER DIMOCK, *A Short Rhetoric for Leaving the Family.*
COLEMAN DOWELL, *Island People.*
    Too Much Flesh and Jabez.
RIKKI DUCORNET, *The Fountains of Neptune.*
    The Jade Cabinet.
    Phosphor in Dreamland.
    The Stain.
WILLIAM EASTLAKE, *Lyric of the Circle Heart.*
STANLEY ELKIN, *Boswell: A Modern Comedy.*
    The Dick Gibson Show.
ANNIE ERNAUX, *Cleaned Out.*
LAUREN FAIRBANKS, *Sister Carrie.*
LESLIE A. FIEDLER,
    Love and Death in the American Novel.
RONALD FIRBANK, *Complete Short Stories.*
FORD MADOX FORD, *The March of Literature.*
JANICE GALLOWAY, *Foreign Parts.*
    The Trick Is to Keep Breathing.
WILLIAM H. GASS, *The Tunnel.*
    Willie Masters' Lonesome Wife.
KAREN ELIZABETH GORDON, *The Red Shoes.*
PATRICK GRAINVILLE, *The Cave of Heaven.*
JOHN HAWKES, *Whistlejacket.*
ALDOUS HUXLEY, *Antic Hay.*
    Point Counter Point.
    Those Barren Leaves.
    Time Must Have a Stop.
TADEUSZ KONWICKI, *A Minor Apocalypse.*
    The Polish Complex.
EWA KURYLUK, *Century 21.*
DEBORAH LEVY, *Billy and Girl.*
OSMAN LINS, *The Queen of the Prisons of Greece.*
ALF MAC LOCHLAINN, *The Corpus in the Library.*
    Out of Focus.
D. KEITH MANO, *Take Five.*
BEN MARCUS, *The Age of Wire and String.*
DAVID MARKSON, *Reader's Block.*
    Springer's Progress.
    Wittgenstein's Mistress.
CAROLE MASO, *AVA.*
HARRY MATHEWS, *Cigarettes.*
    The Conversions.
    The Journalist.
    Tlooth.

    20 Lines a Day.
JOSEPH MCELROY, *Women and Men.*
ROBERT L. MCLAUGHLIN, ED.,
    Innovations: An Anthology of Modern &
    Contemporary Fiction.
JAMES MERRILL, *The (Diblos) Notebook.*
STEVEN MILLHAUSER, *The Barnum Museum.*
    In the Penny Arcade.
OLIVE MOORE, *Spleen.*
NICHOLAS MOSLEY, *Accident.*
    Assassins.
    Children of Darkness and Light.
    Impossible Object.
    Judith.
    Natalie Natalia.
WARREN F. MOTTE, JR., *Oulipo.*
YVES NAVARRE, *Our Share of Time.*
WILFRIDO D. NOLLEDO, *But for the Lovers.*
FLANN O'BRIEN, *At Swim-Two-Birds.*
    The Best of Myles.
    The Dalkey Archive.
    The Hard Life.
    The Poor Mouth.
    The Third Policeman.
FERNANDO DEL PASO, *Palinuro of Mexico.*
RAYMOND QUENEAU, *The Last Days.*
    Pierrot Mon Ami.
ISHMAEL REED, *The Free-Lance Pallbearers.*
    The Terrible Twos.
    The Terrible Threes.
REYOUNG, *Unbabbling.*
JULIÁN RÍOS, *Poundemonium.*
JACQUES ROUBAUD, *Some Thing Black.*
    The Great Fire of London.
    The Plurality of Worlds of Lewis.
    The Princess Hoppy.
LEON S. ROUDIEZ, *French Fiction Revisited.*
SEVERO SARDUY, *Cobra* and *Maitreya.*
ARNO SCHMIDT, *Collected Stories.*
    Nobodaddy's Children.
JUNE AKERS SEESE, *Is This What Other Women Feel Too?*
    What Waiting Really Means.
VIKTOR SHKLOVSKY, *Theory of Prose.*
JOSEF SKVORECKY, *The Engineer of Human Souls.*
CLAUDE SIMON, *The Invitation.*
GILBERT SORRENTINO, *Aberration of Starlight.*
    Crystal Vision.
    Imaginative Qualities of Actual Things.
    Mulligan Stew.
    Pack of Lies.
    The Sky Changes.
    Splendide-Hôtel.
    Steelwork.
    Under the Shadow.
W. M. SPACKMAN, *The Complete Fiction.*
GERTRUDE STEIN, *The Making of Americans.*
    A Novel of Thank You.
PIOTR SZEWC, *Annihilation.*
ESTHER TUSQUETS, *Stranded.*
LUISA VALENZUELA, *He Who Searches.*
PAUL WEST, *Words for a Deaf Daughter* and *Gala.*
CURTIS WHITE, *Memories of My Father Watching TV.*
    Monstrous Possibility.
DIANE WILLIAMS, *Excitability: Selected Stories.*
DOUGLAS WOOLF, *Wall to Wall.*
PHILIP WYLIE, *Generation of Vipers.*
MARGUERITE YOUNG, *Angel in the Forest.*
    Miss MacIntosh, My Darling.
LOUIS ZUKOFSKY, *Collected Fiction.*
SCOTT ZWIREN, *God Head.*

Visit our website: www.dalkeyarchive.com

Dalkey Archive Press, ISU Campus Box 4241, Normal, IL 61790–4241; *fax* (309) 438–7422